Awaken by Love

Awaken by Love

A Novel By

Virginia Raynor

authorHOUSE®

AuthorHouse™
1663 Liberty Drive
Bloomington, IN 47403
www.authorhouse.com
Phone: 1-800-839-8640

First published by AuthorHouse   09/09/2011

ISBN: 978-1-4670-2485-3 (sc)
ISBN: 978-1-4670-2513-3 (ebk)

Library of Congress Control Number: 2011915743

Printed in the United States of America

Any people depicted in stock imagery provided by Thinkstock are models, and such images are being used for illustrative purposes only.
Certain stock imagery © Thinkstock.

This book is printed on acid-free paper.

Contents

Dedication

This book is dedicated to my son. Even though your father has kept us apart, you know deep in your heart how I feel. I love you with every breath of my being. I hope that you grow up to be the best possible "MAN" you can be.

Also to the miracle that blessed my life.

Acknowledgements

First and foremost, I would like to thank God, my Lord and Savior Jesus Christ for giving me the strength to give back.

Thanks to you, the readers that have supported me. A special thank you, to my biggest supporter, K. Puckett. You don't know how much you encouraged me to keep pushing. (Smile). Ms. Sandra Roberts, you are truly God's send. Thank you from the bottom of my heart. Eric Gooden and Alicia Mays for being an extra set of eyes. Kim "Lil Kim" Allen Jr., thanks young blood. Good looking out for your cuz, much appreciated. Martha "Marti" Massenberg, thanks girl. Thanks to both of you guys for being professional and making my vision a reality. Thank you, Alvin "Big Man" Collins for the photography. You always come through right on time.

Prologue

Flashing back on the situation, Ebony should have let her aunt kill Lawrence's ass. See, in 01' after the jail episode, Lawrence whipped Ebony's ass again. He wanted to go see his new girlfriend; (this was one of many in all the years they were married) and decided to take it out on Ebony. She could always tell when he had someone else. The fights became frequent and more intense. He would start an argument for no apparent reason, just so he could leave the house.

As they were in the kitchen, Ebony decided to speak her mind. She knew it would be some kind of repercussion, but didn't care. Ebony was tired of letting the neighbors hear him go off; breaking shit up and whipping her ass, without her trying to fight back.

"You always do the same ole` bullshit. I've been making sure this family thrives, while you support someone else. If you care so much about whoever she is, pack your shit and leave. I do better without your ass anyway. When you are here, it's like taking care of another child. An added mouth to feed! When we are up against the wall and I can't do it by myself, my mother bails us out. Your mother talks shit like you do, but never help. All she got is mouth! You got a nerve buying a bitch cigarettes and lunch, while I am busting my ass to make sure you have. I buy your cigarettes! I eat choke and slide sandwiches when necessary.

I go without! What the hell are you doing? This family comes first in my book, not a trick. You don't take money out the house; you are supposed to put it in the damn house. I am really getting sick of providing for you. You nag just like a fucking woman, but never do your damn part! And you call me a bitch all the time," she said.

Lawrence just stood there and never said a word. She was caught off guard and didn't even see it coming. He slapped the shit out of her. The blow came with a stinging daze. It felt like a bee sting in the middle of July. As she made her way near the stove, trying to go for a kitchen knife; Lawrence then pushed her head hard into the range hood. Bowwww! That shit felt like getting hit in the head with a 2 x 4. The force of the blow made a permanent dent in the appliance. At that point, all she could see was stars and think of the pain and throbbing pressure. She could feel a big ass knot forming on the back of her head. Lawrence goes into the refrigerator and gets the pitcher of lemonade, goes in the cabinet gets a glass and strolls over to the table and pours a glass. This son of a bitch didn't care; he was sipping on some lemonade like it was a reward for a job well done and Ebony was all fucked up. In all actuality, she was telling his ass the fucking truth.

The knot was becoming very noticeable over the course of the hour. As usual she was under so much stress her hair had fallen out. She had been keeping the boy low cut due to the duress. If she did have long hair, a plug would have fallen out right then and there. Scared, Ebony didn't call the police. As usual he always threatened to lie. "Call the police, all I am going to do is lie so you can get locked up again", he said. She ran around the corner of the house into the living room and grabbed the phone off the end table. He remained in the kitchen calm as a cucumber. The smug muthafucker! This time she needed help and in a big way, she called her mother. Granted she was far away, but Ebony needed someone to talk to at that moment.

"Mommie, he was fighting on me again! My head hurts, I can't call the police! I am scared, I will get locked up again", Ebony cried to her mother. Vanessa was fuming mad. "I can't get there baby, but I am sending some help for you. I told him when ya'll got married, never to put his hands on my child. I would never interfere, but he has taken this a little too far. You need to bring your ass home. If you don't move by December, I will come and get a U-Haul and move you myself," Vanessa said.

After getting off the phone, she went upstairs and tried to get herself together. She laid across the bed afraid that she would be attacked again for calling home or pass out from the blow to head. The pain was so severe, all Ebony could do was cry a river of tears.

It felt like an eternity to her, but within four hours the doorbell rang. In came the cavalry from Baltimore! This time it was Ebony's real father's (RL) side of the family. Aunt Ally, Christal, Cory and Jordan. Aunt Ally was her father's aunt and had been sick with cancer. She strolled in with an oxygen tank. You could see the fumes coming from her head. Christal was her father's sister and hell on wheels. She was tougher than most of the men in the family. Cory was her father's brother and Jordan his cousin. As she let the family in, Lawrence became quiet as a church mouse.

They all went into the family room where Lawrence was sitting in the computer chair. Aunt Ally and Jordan sat on the loveseat, Christal and Cory were on the sofa and Ebony sat in the recliner. Ebony felt relieved and safe because her family was there. Aunt Ally spoke first, "If you ever put your hands on my niece again, I will kill you. I have no problem going to jail. I am getting ready to die anyway." Lawrence never said a word, he knew they meant business. He had never interacted with that side of the family. Ebony talked about them and how they were off the charts! He definitely had her mother's side of the family fooled.

The guys took him in a room and tried chatting with him. You could only hear them and not Lawrence. He never spoke a word. The guys talked about having been to jail for fighting on women. Most of the conversation was about how to treat Ebony. No threats were made. They wanted to make him feel as comfortable as possible. Basically, good guy, bad guy roles. On the other hand, the aunts wanted blood! He must have thought that the guys wanted to fight him, but the secret weapon was Christal.

Christal took Ebony upstairs and examined her head. Christal stated, "I am gonna kill his ass!" Ebony pleaded, "Please don't kill him. I don't want you going to jail. I was already there and didn't like being locked up. Also, his mother will know that I had something to do with it, if he came up missing." Christal didn't want to hear anything of the sort. "Look at your fucking head girl! He could have killed you. If he wants to fight on women, especially my niece, then he could try that shit on me." She was ready to pump his ass full of hot lead.

Cory and Jordan tried chatting with Lawrence again to see if he wanted to go to the pub around the corner. The boxing fight was scheduled to come on and they wanted to look at it. Since the Richmonds didn't order the pay-per-view bout, they figured why not throw back some beers with the show. Lawrence was scared shitless. "No, I am not interested in going to the pub," he said. The plan was to get him outside so that Christal could kill him, and for the guys to dump his dumb ass in the woods.

That was the first time Ebony ever seen her husband scared. Around her mother's side of the family, she always was made to look like the evil one, when it was actually him. Whenever family was around, they would think that Ebony had all the mouth because Lawrence was always so quiet. Total deception!

Lawrence never left the house with them, and told the family that he didn't mean to hit her. Ebony had been arguing with him and things got out of hand. It would never happen again. She had heard that shit so many times before. Ebony knew deep down she didn't start anything, this motherfucker was flat out lying. She was just speaking her mind. Ebony had taken this cheating thing for far too long. And to make matters worse, he was providing for someone else. She was sick of being sick and tired.

The family took him at his word. The next day things had calmed down and Christal took their son, Shawn with her back to Baltimore. She wanted to give Ebony and Lawrence time to try and work this thing out. Christal made it a point that she did not want to have to return there due to the fighting. If she did, it would not be a pretty sight!

Once the two were alone, things really didn't get worked out. It was just if they were co-habiting in the house. The only thing that Ebony was good for was sex. Lawrence never spoke a word to her, only when he wanted to get his freak on. "You don't fuck me on the regular. I'd rather pay a whore! She won't talk back," he said. Ebony was getting tired of the bullshit. Why would she want to sleep with his ass after all that had transpired?

This nigga was stupid! He had just whipped her ass and now wanted to fuck. Some people get down like that; probably a thrill for them, but getting fucked up and then having sex wasn't in her character. Make up sex is supposed to be the best ever, but how many times did she have to fall for that. All these ass-whippings and Ebony supposed to keep giving into his needs? She wasn't there just for his sexual pleasures or to be his punching bag. She was his wife. They made vows "til death do us part," but damn it, she wasn't ready to die and not by his hands. That was not part of the deal!

Chapter 1

Fast forward-December 8, 2002

Around two o'clock the movers finally showed up. They had excuse after excuse why they were late. The two of them should have been there by eight o'clock in the morning; that was the damn plan. They couldn't get the truck til 1 o'clock and that truck caught a flat tire on the way to Ebony's house. Ebony didn't want to hear that shit, she wanted to fucking leave. She remembered Lawrence telling her "I ain't leaving, you can fucking leave!" They both had agreed on selling the house and splitting things down the middle, when she returned home the first time if things didn't work out. She wasn't going to wait for that day to happen, because at the rate the relationship was going; he would kill her before that ever took place. Ebony had to get out of there with the quickness!

Ebony had already taken precautions and would tell anyone around her that if something ever happened to her, it was because of her husband. She really thought that he was trying to collect on her life insurance policy. Ebony was never gonna let that happen either. Once she knew that she had gotten the job in Baltimore, she changed her policy over to Miko. Lawrence had received all the money he was gonna get out of his wife and not a penny more. She had done more for him than his own no-good mooching family.

1

It seemed like things were moving in slow motion. These assholes were just standing on the inside of the truck. All Ebony could do to move this process along was to start moving the boxes outside; technically all they had to do was add the boxes on the truck. As she entered back into the house to take a quick look around to see what else she could grab, Ebony came across the surround sound system. She wanted desperately to take her stereo, but the speakers were mounted to the walls in the family room. It was too many cords to disconnect and she couldn't figure it out. "Damn it! Keep moving girl," she thought to herself. One better she took over two hundred cds. If she was leaving with nothing else, the music was going. This had been her passion since a child. She also clipped the first television she had brought his ass (a pic in a pic).

It hadn't even been a good thirty minutes when Lawrence pulled up into the driveway. The sound of the tires squealing, alerted her. Ebony knew that this was going to get ugly and real quick. As he ran in the house and looked around, "Bitch, what the fuck are you doing, you took my tv." He had seen her packing boxes for a month, but didn't know when she was leaving. Guess he figured she was just talking shit again. The day was realization day nigga!

Everything leading up to getting out of there was coming to a halt. "Damn moving men, for being late," she thought. Lawrence blocked the entrance of the door, so Ebony couldn't get out the house. Ebony never said a word. She continued to grab the last little bit of stuff she had in front of her. Fuck whatever else that didn't make it on the truck. She thought to herself, "Muthafucker, I'm leaving you the house and mostly everything in it. Be grateful! I shouldn't have left you shit."

The first time she had left his ass, she took mostly everything down to the kitchen. This included the guest bedroom furniture, the living room and the dining room furniture. Considering everything was in her name anyway, who the fuck was he to tell her what she could and couldn't take. Instead of him trying to buy women for pussy, he should have been an honorable man and took care of his own family, (her and Shawn). Not the other way around! The only thing that saved his ass this time was Vanessa. She told Ebony don't worry about the materialistic shit, you will get all that stuff all over again. Just bring your ass home!

Ebony yelled out to the truck and told the movers to wrap it up. Let's go! Lawrence approached her with hate in his eyes. Ebony was somehow filled with courage. That look was not going to bother her again. She looked right back at him with the same venom and said, "No need to change the locks this time, the key is on the counter. You can have whatever bitch you desire." As she brushed passed him out the front door, he couldn't believe that she had that much guts. She felt like, "Yeah, what a relief I can leave him now. The way he looked at me was like he wanted to beat my motherfucking ass."

It was nothing but "**grace and mercy**" that she made it out of that piece alive. I will survive by Gloria Gaynor played in her head, as she walked to the truck. As she pulled away from the door, all she felt was relief. Once again, she had been saved by the "**Most High**." She had finally escaped the drama!

Ebony had made it out of that abusive ass relationship with her life. She was finally free from the pain and heartache of a no good motherfucka trying to bring her down. Ebony's mind was awestruck! She didn't know what to do or to think. She had to snap her ass back to reality and quick, if she was going to make that journey back home. Subsequently; these fuckers were driving extremely slow. It was bad enough they came late, now everyone was gridlocked in heavy ass rush hour traffic on I-64.

Things just started to go downhill from there. Already agitated, tired and really in need of sleep, this couldn't be happening! It hadn't even been a good twenty miles yet when Ebony saw them put on the blinker to pull over. As she followed them off the exit into Hampton and they pulled under a bridge, she wanted to know what the hell was going on. The driver stated that he was tired and needed some sleep. Ebony wasn't trying to hear that shit. She had been up since o'dark hundred and pumping on adrenaline. She was supposed to have been in Baltimore, or at least half way there before Lawrence stupid ass ever returned home. They had her schedule fucked up. The other guy could see that she wasn't playing with them. She had already given them half of the money too! The time for playing games was over. From that point on, Ebony was going to be calling the shots. "Fellas, the next stop we making will be Kings Dominion, my halfway point. Everyone could use the bathroom and get gas," Ebony stated. The plan was to do just that and they proceeded!

It didn't take that long for them to reach Kings Dominion about an hour and a half. She guessed it was because of the traffic during that time of day. As they all gassed up and used the restrooms, Ebony was ready to get her journey over with. An hour and a half to go . . . .

Getting into Baltimore was taking its sweet lil ole' time. It was like everything was moving in slow motion, like the "Matrix." The phone rang breaking the silence in the car. Ebony was like "Hello," "Lawrence is my man, and he loves me," the caller spoke. Ebony was like "Sweetie, he is all yours." (Click) She felt nothing at the moment; whoever the girl was could have that ass! All Ebony could do was smirk at the situation at hand. That was a childish game to play! She wasn't going back and you could bet your life on that one! She had endured one too many ass-whippings from that nigga. Ebony had been Lawrence's rock, his backbone and this is what he opted for over a good woman.

No real man in his right mind would have given another woman his wife's phone number anyway. This wasn't the first time, but it sure enough would be the last. Of all the times Ebony was out in the streets providing for her family; she never would do no dumb shit like that. A nigga better not have had called her husband with no stupid shit. She would have put his ass in check. The guys Ebony dealt with knew the deal. If you couldn't hang, then get ghost.

The words of her mother resonated in her head again, "you don't know what I had to do to get you what you needed." Ebony was about business in the street to provide for her family, including her dumb ass husband. Mainly it was for Shawn, since his father never stepped up to the plate. Ebony always had to find someone that had her and Shawn's back. On the other hand, she was about protecting her family at all cost. See; role reversal!

Ebony knew deep in her heart, Elizabeth had raised him to be the bitch he was. The only boy with six sisters and acted just like one of them. That is probably why he always called Ebony a bitch. Lawrence was always mad because he couldn't compete with his wife for the top ranking as a real woman. Him and his no good trick that liked playing childish games deserved each other. Good riddance!

Entering into DC, the snow was coming down hard. Ebony ain't have no fuckin music on, just riding with getting home on her mind. "Damn snow coming heavy as shit!" She wanted this day over with quick, fast and in a hurry. It had never taken her this long to get home before.

The phone rang again and snapped her out of her frustration. Leroy called to see how far out she was. Ebony could see light at the end of the tunnel, but was not close enough. Normally she would have put the Beamer on cruise control and glided, but she had these idiots following her. Also, I-95N was getting pounded. Time was moving slow or actually like standing still. As she saw the signs getting close to I-695, her mind was telling her to get the hell off of I-95, girl! Ebony was getting ready to take her chances on 695, just to get there quicker.

Around eight thirty, she finally arrived at her new residence. As she pulled in the parking lot, all she wanted to do was cry. All the trouble she had been in and today's long activities had her exhausted. Ebony knew this wasn't over yet. She had to climb those three flights of stairs to her new life. See when Ebony went for the job interview, she got a place too. She wasn't moving home with Vanessa just yet; Ebony needed time to see if she could make it on her own.

As she pushed the door open to her apartment, her family was inside waiting. They had made themselves comfortable and had been playing spades on the kitchen counter. Everyone started hugging, but it was no time for that until they got rid of the moving men. After the short embrace, they got to business unloading the truck. While outside, her cousin stated, "Glad to have you home cuz." The emotions ran thru Ebony, and she finally broke down and cried. "Seventeen years cuz and I finally made it back home safely," as she gripped her cousin tight.

The movers were worthless; they didn't even bring a fucking box into the house. For all that, Ebony could have moved her own self. She did everything anyway on one end and the family on the other. What were they even there for? Ebony knew how to drive a moving truck, shit! As the family was moving things off the truck and had got the last box off; downstairs in the hallway, her grandmother, Barbara paid the remaining payment to the movers.

Ebony's grandmother never knew about the bullshit, but once she found out she insisted that she come home. Ebony couldn't pay the entire bill because of her expenses. So grandma paid the rest. That was a huge fuckin relief and greatly appreciated. Barbara thanked them for getting her granddaughter there safely. From that point on, the movers disappeared into the night.

Ebony was so relieved to see her people support her. The only person that was missing was her mother. Vanessa was working and couldn't take off. The family stayed about two hours and decided it was time to go. They had been a tremendous help. They put her dining room in place, set up her bed and placed the boxes in the rooms as they were labeled.

The quietness in the apartment as everyone left, gave her a sigh of relief. Ebony had finally did it; she left that ass. Somewhere a sudden burst of energy emerged, before you knew it; it was two thirty and every box was emptied. Ebony had been up for twenty-two hours; but it was well worth it! The bed was made and all she needed now was a hot shower and SLEEP. She did just that.

Awakening to the bright and morning sun, Ebony had a peaceful and much needed rest. It was like a tranquil windfall had graced her presence and she felt instant relief. The relief from the drama, fighting, and being called a BITCH everyday. No more sleeping on Diva and Deja's floor or going to Denny's in the middle of the wee morning hours; scared as hell to stay home. She basically slept with one eye open when she did stay there. All gone!!

This girl had truly been blessed and delivered out of that bondage Lawrence had placed her in. (THAT SHAM OF A SO-CALLED MARRIAGE.) The sad part about it was Shawn had to witness all that abuse and he was stuck with the bastard.

Ebony began to think in deep thought, "My baby should be here. Shawn had stated he wanted to come when I left again. That is why I got two bedrooms. Whatever Lawrence said to Shawn the week before, made him scared to leave. When I told him, we were leaving; he all of a sudden wanted to stay with his father. Granted I stated Shawn could stay to get the divorce papers signed, but I had no intentions on leaving without him. Lawrence didn't uphold to anything that he ever agreed to, so why should I." As she snapped out of her thought, she got dressed and went to the grocery store.

Ebony had two weeks to unwind and collect her thoughts before starting her new job. This would give her time to spend with her mother and stepfather. The reunion with Vanessa was bittersweet. Proud and glad at the same time that her daughter made it home in one piece, but also mad that it took her so long since she was being abused.

Ebony had done a good job at hiding the abuse and masking the pain for a long time. It wasn't til the last few years that she began to tell her mother. Leroy had sensed something, but couldn't put his finger on it.

There first outing as a family was to the furniture store. Three days after arriving; since Vanessa had told her daughter to leave everything in Virginia, she needed a living room set to sit on. Lawrence must have thought that Ebony would fall through the cracks, but Vanessa wasn't gonna let it go down like that. That shit she had was nothing that Vanessa wouldn't and couldn't buy her child all over again. She couldn't buy her life back though, if Lawrence had killed her child.

After arriving to the store, Ebony first tried to get credit on her own. She was just the proud person that her mother raised her to be. Waiting to see if the credit was approved, they looked around the store. Finding out that her application for credit was being denied because of too many delinquencies, made Ebony mad as hell. Ebony never paid anything late, but that fucking Lawrence did and again fucked up her perfect credit.

Vanessa told her daughter don't bother, she had it. That wasn't the point; Ebony just always tried to do the right thing. That's all she ever did. It wasn't in her character to be evil. This sort of thing is what made her gullible all the time, her kindness. Lawrence had taken full advantage of her everything! From her kindness to her finances. This left Ebony in a huge bind.

Once leaving the store, she placed a called to his stupid ass. To her surprise, he answered the fucking phone. Of course he had some slick shit to say. "You knew I had bad credit when you met me." Ebony couldn't believe her ears. On the other hand, yes she could. Her and her family always had taken care of her and her husband. This was typical Lawrence bullshit.

She started yelling thru the phone that once again her mother had to come to her rescue. To top it off, what made matters worse is when he came out his mouth and said "Your mother can get it for you." Then he hung up the phone. At that point, Ebony was ever so grateful to her mother for all the kindness she had shown. That's what mother's do!

Out of all the times Lawrence would say to her "that's how come you and your mother don't get along!" Ebony knew that he was just plain stupid or crazy. Ebony and her mother were tight, more like sisters than mother and daughter. Ebony wasn't scared to tell her mother her opinion about her husband. Be it right or wrong, she had a voice. She had married Lawrence and had to deal with him, and her mother respected her decision. Ebony thought he would say that because he wouldn't say anything to his mother. Lawrence let Elizabeth or anyone else talk shit about his wife. He never did stand up for Ebony, not that she couldn't handle herself!

Lawrence was only a man because of what he had in his pants, that didn't necessarily make him a strong one. He always gave off the impression that he was in competition with Ebony for some apparent reason. That is what women do with other women, not the kind of thing you would do with your spouse. The partnership should have been at least fifty-fifty!

Hindsight being twenty-twenty, the shit really didn't start getting thick until they actually moved to Virginia. His control had weakened and Ebony had begun her independence. No matter how hard he tried to break her, she kept pushing forward. This girl always had a set of goals for herself and tried her damnedest to achieve them. Lawrence wanted her to depend solely on him. How could she when he didn't want to make sacrifices for his family? Someone had to step up to the plate and be the man! That's exactly the role she played.

If she would have just submitted and followed his instructions, Ebony probably wouldn't be in this mess. That was not the person that her mother reared. All Ebony kept thinking about were the signs in the beginning. None of this would have happened if she left him alone back then. Thinking on it at the moment, she would have gladly let someone else take her place. Not that she wished abuse on anyone over the course of time, but she wouldn't have to endure all the years that had been stripped away from her. Ebony only wanted love with someone; a true and dear person that always would have her best interest at heart, and to treat Ebony like the queen she was.

Before you knew it, the two weeks before starting work had come to a close. Vanessa had also worked for the same company almost 19 years. Not saying that she pulled any strings to get her daughter a job there, but Ebony did damn well during the interview process herself. It was off to work as a supervisor, managing assistant living homes.

The first day Ebony felt a little nervous because it was new surroundings. The staff was most pleasant and welcomed her. The director had come through the ranks with Vanessa and knew that if Vanessa could maintain and be a valuable employee, then her baby girl would do the same. The company needed someone reliable and dependable to look out for their clients with special needs, and Ebony fit the bill.

Ebony had plenty of time to reflect on what mistakes she had made and the things that she didn't want to repeat in the next relationship. She was looking forward to a new beginning: different people, places and new adventures on the horizon for this young lady. *"It could only get better from here"*, she thought.

Chapter 2

Christmas was right around the corner and all Ebony could think about was Shawn. She hated thinking about him not growing up with his mother, but she was at a point in her life she had to do what was best for her at that particular moment. Technically she was tired of fighting. She had no more will power in her.

Her ex-boyfriend, Kim had stated to her when she put him out and went back with Lawrence, "Don't use your child as an excuse to go back! You have to do what is best for you. One day your child will get older and leave you." As the thought crossed her mind, things possibly would not have gotten any better if she had stayed with Lawrence anyway. Lawrence had proved that when she went back. The goodness that he showed only lasted four months, before he was back to his old tricks again. He just didn't want her with any other man, but he could be with other women. Such a double standard!

Thinking back, Ebony knew she had did Kim wrong. Packing his shit up leaving it at the door was totally not like her. Part of her felt betrayed when he left her under the circumstances she was in, when Lawrence took Shawn and moved him to New Orleans. She had practically begged Kim not to go to New York or either take her with him. Kim had dismissed her feelings, knowing the stress she was under when she did not know where her son was. Ebony was consumed by the problems of Shawn being gone at that point and this made her decision much easier to put Kim's shit out. He was not there for her when she needed him the most.

Ebony also couldn't help but to think that she would have turned into Lawrence around Kim. All the girl's eyes lusted after him when the two were together. Being that she already had trust issues, Ebony was scared that she would start with the control, jealousy and possessiveness that plagued her in her relationship with Lawrence. Kim didn't deserve what she did to him, but if only he could understand that she didn't want to bring all her baggage into what they had. He had every right to leave her door open and walk the hell out without shutting it. Who could really blame him? Once again always thinking of everyone else and not herself! After the thoughts ran through her mind, she thought of how much of a fool she was back then. If only! I guess you live and you learn!

After a long draining day at work, Ebony just wanted to hit the shower and relax. As she browsed through the cable listing, she stopped at this movie called "ENOUGH". Damn if Ebony hadn't had enough! As she continued watching the movie, damn if Jennifer Lopez hadn't rocked that movie out and became Ebony's hero. Deep down inside, if Ebony had of seen that movie while with her husband, she would have tried everything in her power to get up the courage and kill him herself. She too was fighting for the survival of her child. The mental anguish, acting out and talking back to Ebony from Shawn was all Lawrence's encouragement. Ebony could only come to the conclusion that "Enough" was a movie and not her reality. Her ass would have ended up in jail for life this time. She could see the police gathering her finances, stating she killed his ass cause of the debt that had been occurred. Only for Lawrence to win still. NOT!

What a joyous occasion Christmas should have been at her grandmother's house. Granted Ebony was now amongst family, she was still hurting from not being with Shawn. During the time she was there, she was always torn when it came to him. The hurt and the disappointment of how he behaved, part of her knew that it was Lawrence's doing. As the family gathered around the table this year, no one was missing but Shawn. The family could have cared less about Lawrence, but Shawn would always be a part of the family.

To ease Ebony's mind, the family gathered around the phone like they used to do when she lived apart from them. They all called Shawn to see how his Christmas was coming along; needless to say Lawrence would not answer the phone. Ebony became very depressed, but knew that Lawrence liked making her feel bad. Misery loves company!

He had some serious control issues. Have you ever seen a person that has someone else, but like making your life hell? Lawrence with a capital L! "You thought the grass was greener on the other side," Ebony kept thinking.

During her trip back to the apartment, Ebony felt like a knife had been aimed at her heart. She was trying to get pass the hurt and pain. Visions of the past began to pop in her mind. She remembered the first time Lawrence choked her. The devil was looking her in the face at the point. His true colors really began to show and she saw what he was capable of. He had promised Ebony that this type of thing would never happen again.

Ebony should have been smarter at that moment, to get her shit and get the fuck out of there. After a man hit you the first time, it won't stop unless you put a stop to it! She should have grabbed her baby and fled at that moment. All the thoughts ran through her mind. If she wasn't in the military, she could have returned home with no problem. The dilemma was that she was in the military and she wasn't

13

thinking about going AWOL. Boy how people say shoulda, coulda, woulda! Why didn't someone talk some sense into her then? Maybe she wouldn't feel the pain she felt on such a joyous occasion, which is supposed to be filled with love.

Deep inside Ebony felt ashamed to admit it to anyone. The person that she took her vows with could just snap at a moment's notice. Why try to ruin her life? She had never been married before, but he had. Why put her thru this traumatic experience; for control purposes? All sorts of questions flooded her mind. He was filled with rage, low self-esteem and jealousy. She tried to shake the visions from her mind.

During the course of the night as she went to sleep, she began to toss and turn more. Thoughts of Lawrence kept clouding her mind. "Bitch, Shawn can say what he wants to you! You ain't nobody. Say another word and I will fuck you up!" She tried hard to wake herself up. This was a nightmare, but technically she was just reliving what really happened.

As she finally arouse out of her sleep, she was sweating profusely. All she could do was cry. Ebony felt like shit for letting this behavior go on for so long. When she finally did try to get help from the military, they took Lawrence's side because she had become a civilian. No justice there! As long as you were one of them they could help, when you left after giving them your years of service; they were practically finished with you. Wow!!

Ebony just wanted to remove all the feelings of Shawn out of her life. One minute she resented him. On the other hand, technically he was only a child. Shawn had been brainwashed by a monster. He didn't know any better, which was something that Ebony would have to learn over time. Shawn was just doing what he was taught to do. This just made her hatred towards Lawrence worse. Maybe one day she would forgive him for what he had done. That day wasn't gonna be today!

Ebony began to bury herself into work and schooling. She had begun taking online courses to complete her degree. He had tried to break her concentration while in Virginia, but she wasn't gonna let him get the best of her now that she was gone. Sheer determination to finish what she had started was in the back of her mind. With online courses, you had to be disciplined and organized. Just because you didn't see the classroom didn't mean that your homework, quizzes, mid-terms and finals weren't due. It was hard work, but Ebony was determined to finish.

Finally in January 2003, she received her divorce decree by mail. Ebony had filed in October of the previous year and she was waiting for that motherfucker to go through. Happy New Year BITCH!! Cause she know he got his too!! She couldn't believe that she was now divorced from this living devil here on earth. Things could now get better and she could move forward from here on out, or so Ebony thought.

Good thing she made him pay for half of the divorce. She should have gotten all the money from him. Ebony had paid for his first divorce and also the one that her mother had paid for, for the two of them. He should have paid the whole amount for this one. The best thing that she got out of the deal was her maiden name back. (Washington) Why would she want to keep the name that brought her so much grief?

People say that the devil is busy! In the midst of working a hectic schedule and being on call 24/7, plus schooling, she wasn't prepared for what would happen next. Ebony had thought that she was free and clear, but trouble was brewing around the corner. Everyone has a breaking point. Trouble and turmoil continually lurked at her door. If it wasn't one thing it was always another. It came back to back. This was going to be detrimental and knock the breath out of Ebony.

Being glad to just be home amongst family, and now this. Vanessa had been complaining for years about acid reflex. Finally she would see what her problem truly was. The day of her cousin's wedding, Ebony, Vanessa and Hershell, Vanessa's current boyfriend was off to the doctor's office. Vanessa was having a procedure to see what was wrong with her stomach. As she was lead in the back, Ebony went outside to get some air. Just chilling outside and then in the cafeteria, Hershell found Ebony. He stated that the doctor wanted to speak with her. Ebony went to the office, but the doctor had left. The nurse caught the doctor out back. Ebony was not prepared for what he was going to tell her. Her mother had been diagnosed with stomach cancer. Tears streamed down her face. How in the world was she going to be able to tell her mother when she woke up?

As the three arrived to her aunt's house for the wedding reception, Ebony just kept shaking her head. Vanessa knew something was wrong, because her daughter couldn't look at her without crying. She finally asked Ebony to tell her. As she broke the situation down to her mother, her mother didn't want anyone to know. Ebony would harbor this secret as long as her mother needed her too. Vanessa had always been her protector and she would protect this secret at all cost. For some reason Ebony got herself together. "Leroy had had cancer for years and he was still on this earth. Mommie will be around also," Ebony thought.

Ebony tried to continue to balance work and her studies. Vanessa underwent her first surgery to see if they could remove the cancer. Ebony was just glad that she still had her mother. Vanessa had always been there for her and she was going to do the same. Who else did she have to rely on anyway?

The surgery was a success and life was getting back to normal. Vanessa had to take a disability retirement. She could no longer lift or care for her clients. Technically she probably needed the rest. She had always been a caregiver to someone, now it was time for Ebony to take care of her mother.

In the midst of everything else, things started spinning out of control! Ebony couldn't afford to pay all of her bills. Most of them were when she was married to Lawrence. She needed help! Ebony applied for a consolidation loan, but needed a co-signer because she had only been on her new job for a couple of months. She asked her mother could she co-sign the loan for her. Vanessa was up in debt herself and couldn't help her daughter that time. The only other option was to file bankruptcy. Ebony had to figure out a plan to avoid this measure. Things would have to wait. Ebony would have to buckle down and do the best that she could with what she had.

That's what friends are for! Her homegirl, Deja from VA decided that she was coming to visit. Ebony tried to explain that her funds were short and didn't even have food. Deja was not deterred. She had put into motion that she was going to make the journey to Baltimore to see her friend. Ebony was feeling really down, the girl was used to showing hospitality when a friend or family member came to stay. It cut her down to the core of her heart that she didn't have any food to feed not only Deja, but herself.

Upon arriving, Deja strolled in with a cooler. After the initial hugs, she said "what's mines is yours and yours is mines." Deja had loaded the cooler with meats, coffee, juice and vegetables. Ebony felt ashamed. Deja never paid it any attention. She knew what it was like to finally leave an abusive relationship and start over. The girls had a ball anyway, regardless to the stress on Ebony. Deja made sure of that! Deja not only came to visit with Ebony. She came to handle her own B.I. Ebony however, enjoyed her company immensely.

It had been months now since she had left and Ebony still hadn't heard from Shawn. Ebony and her parents had sent a care package of clothes for Valentine's Day; not a word that Shawn had received the package.

Ebony and her mother decided to take a road trip to see how Shawn was doing. His birthday was around the corner. As they arrived in Virginia, Ebony and Vanessa went to Shawn's school. The bastard hadn't changed any of Shawn's paperwork, because he didn't know any better. The school staff let Ebony have Shawn. Their first stop would be to the court house. While there filing for custody of Shawn, Ebony had Shawn call his father. As he was speaking with him, Shawn said, "Daddy, I am with Mommie." Once he handed the phone back to his mother, Lawrence voice roared through the phone. "I am calling the police and say that you have kidnapped him!" "How can you call it kidnapping when I am still here in Virginia and will return him when you get off work?" Ebony stated.

Ebony, Vanessa and Shawn went to the mall and did all sorts of fun stuff that day. Vanessa was spending money on Shawn like crazy, as she always did. Shawn was so happy to see his mother and grandmother. This was the loving kid that she had help raise since birth. Shawn always had manners and very respectful in front of his mother, only when he was alone with her. You could see a difference in Shawn. He was like a kid in a candy store. Just the attention and affection showed was worthwhile. The time was winding down and it was time to return Shawn.

The three rang the doorbell of the place she once called home. This was the first time she had set foot on this property since the great escape. Lawrence had this mean ass look on his face. The place looked exactly the same. Filled with everything that she left and still dirty. Vanessa tried to break the tension and asked that they order some food.

Sitting in the family room eating before getting back on the road, Lawrence had gone upstairs. While upstairs he persuaded Ebony to join him. As Ebony made her way up the stairs, she knew he was going to try and con her in some way. Before long, her pants were around her waist and he was licking her love pearl. Since she had left him, she hadn't had head given to her like that. That was all he could get out of her. She refused to have sex with him for old time sakes and he obliged to just get what he could. She made her mistake before on that avenue.

While the two was upstairs, Shawn began to tell all to his grandmother downstairs. He stated that he and his father had driven all the way to Philly to see "Aunt Shannon." See Shannon was Ebony's high school girlfriend that stayed with them in 96', due to her drug addiction. Topping that, he was coming to Baltimore that weekend, this was only in a couple of days.

Once Ebony came downstairs, Vanessa whispered in her ear. Ebony couldn't believe her fucking ears. Granted he had been cheating on her while she was still married, but so soon to take her child to Philly to be visiting another woman that was supposed to be Ebony's so called friend.

The pieces of the puzzle were coming together. Right before Ebony left Lawrence, she had seen a phone number in his phone with the name Shan listed. Ebony had asked him who was it. He stated, "A guy on my job." Funny but the calls were starting at eight in the morning after he had left to go to work. Ebony had dialed the number and Shannon was on the other end. She asked; "Why are you calling my husband early in the morning?" Last time Ebony checked, she had kicked her out and Lawrence's sister had done the same. Shannon's excuse was; "to check on Lawrence's family." Bullshit!!

So technically, the first time Ebony had caught the two of them together was when they were home alone and Lawrence was in his bathrobe; he had fucked the slut then. Good thing that all Ebony let him do just now, was lick her pussy. Even that had her disgusted for even letting him do that. He was just a nasty ass dog that would fuck or suck anything that had a crack.

At that instance of finding out about Shannon, Lawrence would be dead in Ebony's eyesight forever. Never ever would she be a fool for his ass again. He definitely wouldn't get no type of play from her ever! He could be the last man on a deserted island with her dog, and Ebony would let her dog do her first. That is how much she despised her ex-husband. Lawrence had chosen her friends to sleep with. He didn't even have the decency to find a woman on his own. Guess they say "Choose the ones that are closer to home, those are the most easiest to conquer!"

Ebony had to get out of there. She had had enough. He still had to continue lying his way through life. As the family was saying their goodbyes to Shawn, Lawrence looked at Ebony's stomach. Since the release of stress he had placed on her was gone, Ebony regained her undaunted figure. Lawrence stated that his current girlfriend was pregnant. This did not deter Ebony, because she knew better. Especially if it was Shannon, then a crack baby was in the making. He couldn't get anyone pregnant; someone had pulled the okey doke on his ass. He wanted so bad to have a baby, he fell for anything. Ebony just smirked. This was another one of his delusional mind tricks. Deep inside; Lawrence really believed what he said out of his mouth. What a fool!!

A couple of weeks later, Vanessa and Ebony were sitting in church one Sunday morning. Vanessa's sister leaned over and started talking to her. After the morning services were over, Vanessa asked Ebony could she keep a secret. Sure! "Your aunt just told me, she seen Lawrence at a birthday party with Shannon in Baltimore!" Fuck that! He was with Shannon. Ebony could have cared less, the issue at hand; where was her baby? The fact that he had Shawn in Baltimore and wouldn't even let him see his mother was outrageous. He didn't even have the decency to call and say they were in town. Shannon's grandmother only lived down the street from Ebony's grandmother. What a dirty bastard? To think that living that close, it would go unnoticed. Ebony was livid!

When she arrived home, she got to work. She started researching on the internet to find that sleazy bitch, Shannon. Ebony just kept thinking, "I let that no good bitch into my home and she fucked my husband (at the time), now he is taking my son to visit her in Philly and Baltimore. I would never have done no shit like that to her. Bitches they take your kindness for weakness! Her time is marked."

She found two numbers that were possibly matches. The first one was a winner. Hello Shannon, Ebony stated! "What is this I hear that my son was in the likes of your company? I have never done no crud ball shit like that to you. How could you do that to me? I took your ass in, and this is how you repay me! Stay your fucking distance. If I ever see you in Baltimore, I don't know if I will hurt you, so stay far away!" Shannon was speechless.

Ebony did one better and hooked Lawrence no good ass on a three way. She wanted to see what he had to say about the situation. As usual he lied. He told Shannon that he had no dealings with Ebony. Ebony knew that was a bold face lie. He had just sucked Ebony's pussy juice like a champ and was not even man enough to admit it. Not to mention that she was at least married to him. His dumb ass would never get the chance another day in his life to even sniff Ebony's ass.

Ebony did what she could to maintain. Times were getting rough and she finally broke down and sought options for bankruptcy. All she could think of, was her credit that she worked so hard for would be destroyed due to him. What other choice did she have? None! She found this lawyer (that turned out to be shady as hell) that told her, that she could put the house in Virginia on her bankruptcy and they would take the house from Lawrence. This was music to her ears!

The Richmonds had agreed that if things didn't work out, they would sell the house. Why should he have a house that her credit got? Ebony began the proceedings for the bankruptcy. Soon his ass would be out the house once and for all. She had been scraping up money to pay the lawyer, but he was always asking for more. Ebony should have known something was up; that bloodsucker wouldn't even let her parents come in to meet him. Then he got mad at her because she wouldn't pay for some kind of credit rebuilding. Why do professionals always try to bleed you dry for their expertise? Women in domestic violence situations always get caught in a catch twenty-two; damned if you do, damned if you don't.

Finally after dealing with him a couple of months the process moved forward. Ebony found herself sitting in the US Bankruptcy Court. She was nervous as hell. After being called, the Commissioner asked her all sorts of questions. The most important one to her, was that she was now divorced and could not afford all this debt that was left from her marriage. The Commissioner asked her, "So what did you get out of the divorce?" "Nothing but my maiden name back." She would have to play the waiting game to see if everything she asked for would be granted.

The decree came and all the debt was demolished, but the house. The fucker escaped again. Ebony would have never filed if the courts wouldn't take the house. The price you pay for shady ass people.

Chapter 3

January 06' had arrived with some unexpected revelations that always comes with the New Year. Vanessa had been really ill, and Barbara was having a church gathering at the house. Vanessa enlisted Ebony to pick her up. She wasn't too thrilled with the church members asking her questions, so she wanted Ebony to take her to her house. When Ebony arrived to her mother's home, Vanessa could barely walk. She had lost a tremendous amount of weight and had no strength. Ebony had been calling and dropping by, but didn't know her mother was suffering in this manner. Ebony finally got her mother to her apartment and tried to make her as comfortable as possible. While there, Vanessa started going through hot and cold changes. Ebony had become concerned and asked if she needed to go to the hospital. Vanessa refused because she felt that if she went, she would have to stay.

Subsequently about eight hours later, Vanessa decided that it was time. Ebony tried to call a couple of people for assistance in getting her mother's clothes on, but to no avail. She did the best she could and then carried her mother to her car, and drove quickly to the emergency room. Vanessa knew all too well; the hospital had admitted her.

Ebony called Lawrence's phone to let Shawn know that his grandmother was really ill. To her surprise, Shawn answered the phone.

Vanessa was ecstatic to hear her only grandchild's voice. Lawrence had been trying to keep Shawn away from Ebony and her family since the divorce. The family had only seen Shawn about three times since then.

Once Vanessa started to cry, Ebony exited the room and had Shawn put his dad on the phone. She pleaded with her ex-husband to bring their child to see his grandmother. Ebony felt that the doctor's prognosis was grave, six months or less. Lawrence stated that it couldn't be that week because he had to work, but the following would be best.

Ebony knew time was running out for her mother. Cancer had taken control of her fragile body and it was starting to wear thin. Vanessa's attitude became unbearable for some, but Ebony pushed forward and didn't care. Everyday she would tell her mother, "not on my watch." One instance, Ebony went to the hospital after work and Vanessa told her to get out. She didn't let that deter her; she was there everyday faithfully. She would pray with her mother and let her know that the "**Almighty**" didn't make mistakes.

Vanessa was preparing herself for death. She would call Ebony and forget why she had called. Vanessa was developing dementia (changes in the brain that causes forgetfulness). Often times it was to let her child know about where her personal information was located. Other times, just to hear her daughter's voice. Ebony didn't mind, because she knew that time was of the essence. It wouldn't be long before she would never hear her mother's voice again. The family had gathered around one day and Vanessa's spirits seemed like they were up. She told everyone that she was going home on the 21st of the month.

Four days later, Vanessa phoned Ebony that morning to see if she was coming up to the hospital. Ebony told her mother yes, but was it an emergency that she needed to be there right away. Vanessa said no. Ebony, Leroy and Barbara had planned a trip to Charlestown, West

Virginia. While traveling Vanessa phoned and asked how come she hadn't arrived there yet? Ebony tried to occupy her mother's mind, because she had told her where she was going. Ebony got on the horn and phoned her aunt to run interference until she could get back. Upon arriving back that night, Vanessa had been moved to the Intensive Care Unit. The whole family had gathered around and Vanessa was able to say her last goodbyes. Ebony's mother had instructed her to let her dogs out, since they had been gone all day.

Ebony ran to the store and then to let Vanessa's dogs out real quick, she received a call, "Your mother stated that she does not want DNR. "What the hell was that?", she thought. Do not resuscitate, the nurse said. Ebony was flying like a bat out of hell back to the hospital. She didn't know what was going on, but that was her mother. The only one she had, and to keep her mother alive was her wish. Once she got back to the room, Ebony talked to her mother. "Why not resuscitate you? You are the only one I have!" Vanessa told her child, "I don't know what I am talking about baby!" She looked at the nurse, "Do whatever my daughter says to do!" Ebony couldn't believe her ears. She was holding on to her mother, til she couldn't anymore. She knew soon it was going to be over, but didn't want to face the facts.

The last three in the room were Ebony, Barbara and Hershell. Vanessa looked at Hershell and gave him a kiss. In all of Ebony's years, she had never seen her mother kiss anyone. That was something that she never did. As he was getting ready to leave, Vanessa said, "You didn't give me a kiss!" Hershell walked back and gave Vanessa a big kiss again. She had forgotten that quick that he had given her a kiss already. Vanessa looked into her daughter's eyes and stated, "Please do what I asked you to do." She also looked at her mother and told her, "I love you." Ebony hugged her mother and reminded her that what "**God**" had for her was for her. Ebony could not stand to see the sight of them putting a breathing tube in her mother, so she left to get some sleep.

The next day, Ebony had taken off from work. She couldn't even open her eyelids, they were glued shut. It was like "**God**" **Himself** had put her in a deep coma like sleep. Later that day, Hershell phoned to say that the doctor's wanted to see her. After arriving at the hospital, the doctor stated that they had done all they could possibly do. Ebony did not want to give up on her mother. She wanted to save her at all cost; this was the only person other than Leroy that ever gave a damn about her.

Ebony and Barbara stood vigil over Vanessa's bed all night long. As Barbara and Ebony were talking, she told Ebony that Vanessa started to sing last night after she left. Vanessa sang her favorite song, "I Won't Complain." Ebony knew at that moment, Vanessa had made her peace with the "**Lord**." She was ready to go home to be with "**Him**." Ebony could not stand to see the shape her mother was in. Vanessa had six tubes running on both sides of her chest and the tube down her mouth. Her chest was heaving up and down with the machine.

Around four o'clock in the morning when the nurse came in, Ebony made a decision to pull the plug. The fluid from the twelve tubes of whatever they were pumping into her mother was going in and nothing was coming out. She believed deep down in her heart, Vanessa would not want anyone to see her body swollen. Vanessa was a fashion goddess and very judgmental about her appearance.

Ebony called her mother's two sisters and Hershell. They all arrived at the hospital around 8:30a.m. The doctor came in and the process began. As the tears escaped Ebony's eyes; she watched the machine pump one last time. FLATLINE!

The family started to hold prayer and sing Vanessa's favorite hymn. Tears of sadness filled the room. Vanessa was gone and it was twenty-one days that she had been in the hospital. She had called it to a tee.

Ebony's first call was to Leroy; he was at work at the moment and rushed to see Vanessa. Ebony also left a message on Lawrence's phone. The two weeks had come and gone without Shawn ever seeing his grandmother alive. She went back into the room and just sat there massaging her mother's feet. It wasn't a question of why, Ebony knew that the **Lord** needed her mother more.

It was surreal, to have your flesh and blood die in front of you. At that moment all Ebony could think of was, "**God**" knows best. Tears were not a factor for her at that particular moment. Ebony had to somehow digest it all and figure out what she was going to do without her best friend. She took off and made it to Vanessa's home. As Ebony went into the closet to get her mother's personal information, she remembered everything her mother had told her to do. "If you don't know where to take my body, ask my mother! People have walked on me my whole life, put me in a mausoleum." Vanessa had said.

About four hours later, Elizabeth called to say that Lawrence would be bringing Shawn to the funeral. At no time did she ever receive a phone call from him. Ebony could not believe that he had no respect to offer his condolence. All that Vanessa had done for him, she had his back more than Elizabeth did. At that point, she wasn't even mad at Lawrence. He was just being simple minded as usual, like he was raised. No class! The fruit don't fall far from the tree.

Ebony stood strong, because that is what her mother instilled in her. She made the arrangements and delegated certain aspects to family members. The day before the viewing, Ebony arrived at the funeral home to make sure her mother was to her satisfaction. Family members wanted to know would she be alright, because at no time did they see her cry. Ebony had stuck by Vanessa's side the entire time and knew that "**God**" knew best. Later that night, Lawrence arrived with Shawn. Ebony's face showed the disgust she had for her ex-husband. She didn't have any words for him that night, so she took Shawn to her apartment. Lawrence stayed at Barbara and Vanessa's home.

It was a beautiful February morning, unusually warm for that time of year; Ebony would see her mother's face for the last and final time. With sorrow filling the air, Lawrence just stared at Ebony with hatred in his eyes. This wasn't even a day for the drama!

As the family entered into the church; Ebony and Shawn were first to see her mother. Shawn broke down because he had not seen his grandmother or mother in about two years. Vanessa was the only grandmother, he knew. That closeness was now lost. Just to see his grandmother lying in a casket was taking a toll on the child.

After returning home, Ebony tried so desperately to have a civil conversation with Lawrence. It seemed like everything that she had said went in one ear and out the other. She stated that he could have called to say that he could not bring Shawn to the hospital. His excuse was he had car troubles, and couldn't make it. "Wouldn't it have been nice for you to communicate that shit!", Ebony said. Ebony would have made provisions to get Shawn up to Baltimore, considering he had been around his grandma Vanessa all his life. She also told Lawrence that Shawn could have the best of both worlds. There was no reason for Lawrence to keep Ebony and her family away from the only family Shawn knew.

As Vanessa's business affairs were handled, Ebony needed to handle some of her own. Ebony had lit a fire up under the lawyer's ass to get the ball rolling on selling the house. It had been two years, and it seem like nothing was going anywhere. It wasn't like he was doing it Pro-Bono! Granted they had struck up an agreement that he didn't get paid until the house was sold, but he was trying to milk it for all that it was worth. During the course of the years, she had made many offers to Lawrence. The first year, to buy her out of her share of the house.

"I don't have the money!" he said. The second year, Ebony offered to give her half to him so that she could move on with her life. "I want to make your life miserable!" he said. He was doing just that! He never paid the mortgage on time and it affected Ebony's credit report in a big way. In order for her to purchase a home of her own, she had to do something.

The death of Vanessa rocked her to the core. Ebony showed great strength during the funeral, but mentally was a nervous wreck. She never let anyone see her cry. Countless nights she would break down and cry. Everyday at work, she couldn't wait to get off. The ritual was to go to the cemetery and chat with her mother. Ebony kept her emotions bottled up inside of her. Til one day she had a vision. Her mother's voice came to her "Why are you crying? Weren't you the one who said that what **GOD** had for me was for me! Get up and get yourself together, I am fine." Ever since that day, a new found outlook emerged.

Often times when you think you are at peace and finally conquered one problem another one arise. Ebony knew in the back of her mind where her strength came from, but didn't know if she could handle it all. After the death of her mother, she took her own advice that helped lift her mother in her final days. "What God has for you, is for you!" She carried herself like the solider she was, tall, strong and proud.

Chapter 4

The following month Ebony made arrangements to get Shawn for the Easter weekend. Thinking that Vanessa had left Ebony money and she would give Shawn some, Lawrence agreed. While driving non-stop to Virginia, she had to go to the bathroom really bad. She had made a promise to herself that she would never return to that house again. It was painful for her to do, with all the bad memories. But, oh no, she had to go! She called Lawrence and stated that she was around the corner and needed to use the bathroom.

The uneasiness Ebony felt as she pulled into the driveway, should have told her something. She had not been in the inside of her house since the supposed kidnapping claim in 03'. The house was filthy and grungy. Ebony thought she would have done better using a McDonald's restroom. Once Ebony saw Shawn that made things worthwhile. Of course Lawrence had an excuse to see her again and to be nosey. He stated that Shawn's clothes were not ready for church yet. He would have to come and bring them to her later.

Ebony made sure that whenever she was in Lawrence's presence, she would be on point and fly. Her hair, nails and clothes always gave the look that said "this is what you've been missing!" Ebony was so ecstatic to see her son. Shawn was growing up quickly. Mother and son spent the day going shopping for his Easter Monday outfit, seeing old friends and dinner.

While at dinner, Lawrence called to see where they were. He was trying to see where they were staying the night, but unfortunately Ebony was smarter. She met him at Captain George's Restaurant. Lawrence had all month or even that week to get Shawn's clothes together. As usual, he just wanted to see her face for some reason. If he felt that way, he wouldn't have abused her and Ebony would still be married to his dumb ass. Oh well!

The next morning mother and son went to breakfast and to Ebony's amazement, Shawn ate like an adult not a nine year old. After getting dressed, they arrived at the church Ebony attended, while living there. Ebony missed her old church, and it was a pleasant surprise when she showed up. She got to see her former church members on the Beautification Ministry. Service was excellent.

She had also planned to see one of her best friends, Diva. Diva had made a lavish Easter meal. Ebony didn't eat from everyone, but Diva's cooking was like her own. Spending some much needed time with her dear friend, it was time to make it to Hampton for yet another dinner. It wasn't like they had not just eaten at Diva's house, but this was going to be the drop off point. Lawrence met them at Grate Steak, and Ebony was pleasantly nice to him. Shawn once again ate like he was an adult. Ebony made mention to Lawrence that he needed to watch Shawn's weight. If he kept at it like he was doing, he was going to be an obese child. She was concerned because Shawn was getting overweight like Lawrence had done since she left him.

Well, it was time for Ebony to get back on the road! Only an overnight with her son, damn she felt bad for leaving him. While on the road, Ebony called Leroy to say that she was on her way home. Tired as she was, she finally made it home safely at four o'clock in the morning.

Prior to the arrival of the summer, Ebony had been looking for a home about three months. She finally found one and was looking to close. During the memorial service (which was her mother's birthday), Ebony had planned on telling her family she was closing the following day.

Ebony had inquired about having Shawn come to visit for the summer. When she phoned Lawrence, he stated that Shawn had to attend summer school. Ebony pushed forward and with the help of Vanessa leaving her money, she purchased the home she wanted. She closed the day after her mother's birthday, which was Shawn's birthday. Ebony thought that this was the greatest gift her mother had given her. Finally a home with warmth and love, not a house filled with demons and drama.

Ebony called to check on Shawn to ask about summer school. Shawn stated, "I been here all summer in the house. I didn't go to no school." This made her really mad. Her son could have been enjoying time with his family in Baltimore. He was being used as a babysitter. Ebony told Lawrence, "Bring my son; you've been using him as a fucking babysitter."

Shawn finally arrived that July while Ebony was at her mother's cleaning out her room. Ebony asked why they had taken so long, Shawn stated because of "her." Ebony wanted to know who "she" was, she asked Lawrence why he would bring a woman and leave her a couple doors down the street and not introduce them. Later she found out from Shawn that his dad had gotten married. And her kids were the ones he was watching. This was a shock to Ebony, because after talking to Lawrence at Vanessa's funeral he stated he would never get married again. She really could have cared less. Her only complaint was that her child was living there. Ebony felt it was only fair to know who was helping to raise her child.

Once Shawn's arrival, it seemed like Lawrence called Ebony's phone every other day. Finally she told him that he had Shawn all this time and wouldn't allow phone conversations or visits, why keep calling? She was Shawn's mother, the only one he knew and she was not going to harm her child.

The summer was slowly slipping away and almost time for Shawn to return home. Ebony decided to call Lawrence and see what Shawn needed for school. The voice on the other end was announced as Mrs. Richmond. Ebony thought it was a big joke. She asked the new Mrs. Richmond, if she didn't think that something was strange that her husband did not introduce them. Taking a three and a half hour trip not to get out the car was a little crazy to Ebony. She could tell that this girl was young. She pushed on with her mission to find out about school items, but got her regular response from Lawrence, "I got it." Ebony brought all of Shawn's school clothing despite what he had said.

The last night with Shawn, she had taken him to see Chris Brown and Ne-Yo. The final morning had come and it was time to take Shawn to Kings Dominion, which would be the drop off point. When Ebony and Shawn arrived at K.D., Lawrence was there. Ebony and Shawn was stuck in traffic which is the only reason Lawrence beat them to the drop off point. Her ex-husband simply stared at his ex-wife as he always did. After collecting Shawn's things, Shawn got in the car and Lawrence pulled off. Shawn didn't want to leave, and Ebony could feel it in the intensity of her child's hug. Ebony dropped a tear as they pulled off, wishing that her baby didn't have to leave.

Missing her son so much, she made a phone call to see how he was doing. On the other end of the phone, was the new Mrs. Richmond again. She made clear to stress that point to Ebony. Ebony never got her first name, but really could care less. As the two chatted, Ebony expressed her concerns about Shawn. The new wife thanked Ebony for all the clothes that she brought Shawn. Ebony didn't need a thanks that was her child. She felt as though that is was really weird that Lawrence would drive this woman to Baltimore, and not even introduce her to Ebony. As the two continued to talk, Ebony could sense the girl probably only needed a place to stay with her kids.

Ebony did the unthinkable; she asked her where the family was planning on living at since that was her house. Mrs. Richmond was dumbstruck, she didn't know that. She told Ebony that they were planning on staying there, that it was Lawrence's. So Ebony broke it down for her. "That is mines, you must don't check the mail. The mortgage comes in my name sweetie!" She was really quiet. The conversation ended with Ebony having a smirk on her face. Lawrence was still lying to the ladies just to get the panties. Let's see how far that relationship would last.

Ebony finally received a court date for the sale of the house in Virginia. Ecstatic that it been about three years now and finally something was gonna be done. She was forcing his ass out of the house. He couldn't pay her and wanted to make her life a living hell. The ball was in his court now. Ebony contacted her faithful friend, Diva to see if she could stay the night to attend court. That wasn't a problem with Diva.

Sunday evening after rush hour, Ebony had already packed her clothes and tried to take a nap. When she realized that she wasn't going to sleep, she decided to hit the road. Once in DC, she finally realized that she had forgotten her clothes. Ebony had her overnight bag with shoes and toiletries. "I tell you this is starting out wrong," she thought to herself. She refused to turn back around, granted she only had $50 to her name. Ebony pulled off the exit and searched for Target. Damn a blouse, cami and a pair of pants $48. What other choice did she have? Ebony couldn't fit Diva's clothes or else she would have saved herself money. Forging ahead, she made it there after midnight.

Ebony remembered Diva always telling her to never park in just a spot except for the visitor's spot. There were none. She circled around twice and finally found a parking spot. Ebony figured she would only be there for about four hours of sleep.

The next morning as Ebony arose and was chatting with Diva, she wanted Ebony to get her son off to the bus stop that morning. Ebony had no problem with it. She went outside to get the flyers for their upcoming dinner they were going to be selling, and low and behold her vehicle was gone! What else could go fucking wrong? Bad enough she didn't really have money to buy a new outfit considering her's was hanging on her door at home. Now the car gone! What about gas? Something good has to come out of all this! Diva had to delay from going to work. Boy was she a good friend! Not only that, she used her rent money to get the car out of the pound. What a blessing!!

Ebony made it to court just in the nick of time. Finally she met her lawyer face to face. Throughout the process, her ex made excuse after excuse. Sitting around the table the look on Lawrence's face, was that he could kill Ebony at that moment. As the proceeding progressed, the Commissioner ordered that the house be sold. Lawrence was not liking the verdict at all. That was his dumb ass fault; he could have had the house free and clear. He wanted to make Ebony pay, so this is what he got! Ebony was a lil fearful, so her lawyer decided to walk her to her car.

Driving up the highway back home, the phone rang from an unknown number. As Ebony answered, "I hope you have good credit, cause you are gonna pay," Mrs. Richmond said. Ebony just hung up the phone. First she was so nice to Ebony thanking her for the clothing, now it was only some summer clothing that Ebony supposedly had purchased! Ebony couldn't get over the fact that she brought her son all his school clothes and they weren't summer clothes either. That is what Lawrence got for lying to her. Why was she calling Ebony anyway? Her husband should have been dealing with Ebony on anything concerning the house or their child. Only his stupid ass once again would give someone her phone number. Now she's starting to get the gist of his wicked ways.

Chapter 5

Throughout the process of selling the house, Lawrence wouldn't let the Commissioner into the house. Business papers showing the second mortgage he had taken out on the house were never provided to the courts. Ebony knew what he had done before she left him the first time, and she was adamant that she wasn't paying for his shit again. She refused to sign her name to it.

The lawyer always suggested that she should be paying upfront charges to cover this or that. Here she was again with shady ass professionals! Why should she? Lawrence had been living there for five years without her and he should have taken care of everything. Three years to get something finally done, the lawyer was sleeping on the damn job. On numerous occasions, it was like he was working for her ex-husband instead of her. No matter when he sent a letter or received a phone call from Lawrence, it was on Ebony's dime. She just wanted the process to be over.

Despite the fact that Lawrence hated her guts, he decided to call her. As Ebony answered the phone, she wanted to know was the call in reference to Shawn. "No this is not about Shawn, it is about the house." Lawrence had another scheme up his sleeve. The next voice she heard was a guy from "We Buy Ugly Houses." Ebony never professed that the house was a mansion, but was a far cry from ugly. What on earth? He told her that he was willing to purchase the house for one hundred and twenty thousand dollars. Even though that was a tempting offer, she explained that the house was under a court order and could not be sold by the parties that owned it. Lawrence was not a happy individual. He hung the phone up on Ebony.

The next ploy he devised was to have the new Mrs. Richmond purchase the home. Ebony's lawyer tried to sway her decision to take the Richmonds up on their offer. Ebony really didn't care as long as they came up with the money to buy her out. The stalling took two weeks without the Richmonds being able to purchase the home. The last and final gimmick was to say that he had a lender. The lawyer acted like he couldn't see that Lawrence was buying time. "Sell the damn thing already! This is costing me money. He had a chance to have it free and clear, didn't want it! Kick that ass out! No more chances," Ebony thought.

Christmas day, Ebony decided to call Shawn to see if he received his gift from her and his great grandmother. "Merry Christmas can I speak to Shawn?" Ebony said. "Shawn, Ebony is on the phone for you." At that instance, Ebony got indignant. Who the fuck was she to tell her son to call her by her first name? That was her child and she better take heed!

As Shawn got to the phone and the pleasantries were shared, Ebony asked her son how was Christmas? Shawn had a sad tone in his voice. Ebony became alarmed. As she asked him what was wrong, Shawn stated that all he had gotten for Christmas was a computer chair and one game. His stepmother's children got everything. Ebony was furious! How dare this motherfucker treat someone else's children better than his own? Typical Lawrence fashion, pussy is better than being a responsible parent. Shawn further explained that he did not receive any gifts from his mother or great grandmother. "Let me speak to your father," Ebony said. Lawrence came to the phone with bullshit excuses about he must hadn't checked the mail. Ebony told him, "I will wait." Out of the blue the gift cards showed up. Shawn would never see that money for himself.

As if things couldn't get any worst! Two days before the New Year, Barbara called Ebony to let her know that she had some mail on the table. As Ebony went to her grandmother's house to retrieve it, it was a court date for Child Support. "That fucker!" For five years Ebony had been trying to talk civilly to that asshole; whenever he would answer the phone. That came far and few in those amount of years. They had agreed on alot of stuff and he never abided by it. Before she left him, they agreed that he didn't get child support and Ebony would not get half of his retirement. Ebony was cool with it. She always kept her promises. Whatever she said she was going to do, she did. Ebony always held up to her end of the bargain, unlike that motherfucker!

In the five years that she had been gone, he hadn't bothered her. Everytime she asked him did Shawn need anything, he always said "I got it." For the few times that Ebony had seen her child in those years, she always sent him home with clothing and shoes. Why the sudden change? Was the new Mrs. Richmond calling the shots now or was it because they were getting kicked out of the house?

Ebony arose at 3 a.m. to get ready to pick up her grandmother. The two ventured down to Virginia in the cold weather. After arriving at the courthouse, and seeing Lawrence, Ebony was disgusted. He looked like an over-weight pit-bull. Before the case was called, they went into a room together for mediation. This is where D.C.S.E. asks for your pay records. Of course, Lawrence didn't have any of his, so Ebony stated the same; although she was thoroughly prepared.

The clerk didn't call the case until 2 p.m. Didn't they know that she had driven all the way from Baltimore? This shit was becoming an inconvenience to her. As the case was beginning, Ebony had all her proof. It was like the judge was dismissing all this information. Lawrence claimed that he didn't know that his wife (Mrs. Richmond) called Ebony and threatened to take her for child support. He also stated to the judge, that he was in total agreement with selling the house. The truth was that Ebony was paying a lawyer to force him out. The only thing the judge asked was that he not damage the house, "Oh, no your Honor," he said. The steam was coming out of Ebony's ears. She couldn't believe this bullshit. "The parent that had the child, had all the rights," she thought. The conclusion was $400 a month, to his no good ass for support payments.

Walking out of the courtroom, her ex had this grin on his face. As Ebony approached him, she said, "I wanna spit on your no good ass, but you are not worth my saliva! You are just mad because I am more man then you will ever be. The only thing that constitutes you as one, is the dick between your legs and you couldn't even use that right!" Barbara couldn't believe how her granddaughter was talking. "Ebony you talk like a sailor!" Ebony informed her grandmother that she was one! She finally had to apologize to her grandmother for her behavior.

A couple of months later, the shocker came when the Commissioner was finally able to gain access to the home. It was in shambles. As the Commissioner walked around and begun taking pictures, it was an estimate of $60,000 worth of damage. Ebony couldn't believe her fucking eyes of how he let the house get run down like that.

As Ebony thumbed through the download of the pictures, the stove was nasty inside and out; last time she checked there was a one touch self—cleaning button. The grass was so high it touched the power lines; she did leave a lawn mower. He kicked the fence down, pulled the motion detector from the wall. The central ac unit was broken. It was replaced with wall units that left water stains in the walls. He pulled up the pool and busted the sink with a hammer. The shed was filled with trash, like the house. Also, Ebony really believed that the new Mrs. Richmond was just as nasty as her husband, to live like that. Every year he was filing taxes on the house and Shawn. What was he doing with the money? Ebony was going to be in the fight for her life now.

It had taken about two weeks, the day had finally come and Lawrence had moved out of the house. Good, but one small detail was lacking. Ebony didn't know where the hell Lawrence had moved with her son. It was bad enough he destroyed her house, but now this.

The deal wasn't finished yet! Everyone made some money off the deal but Ebony! The Commissioner got his fair share, Ebony's lawyer, all the people that gutted the house, court time and even that bastard Lawrence. Ebony's lawyer sent her a breakdown of all the assets and liabilities. She once again couldn't believe her fucking eyes. Now she was stuck paying half of everything, including his second mortgage he never paid. This made her furious! How the fuck was she responsible for his shit. Bad enough he did all that damage and still walked away with money. Ebony's money went to her lawyer. That's the price you pay when you get hemmed up with a shiesty ass lowlife. What more could she do? Even though she was mad as hell; Ebony got that bitch out of her house. Fuck the money in a sense, she had a new home! With his bad credit, Lawrence wouldn't be able to get much.

Chapter 6

Ebony still hadn't heard from Shawn since they had been put out of the house. According to the divorce decree, Ebony and Lawrence were supposed to exchange addresses if they moved within two days. This had now been a couple of months.

While at work, a co-worker told her about Zaba search. Ebony got hot on the j.o.b and started investigating. She came up with a couple of possible addresses. The first one felt like it was a winner because it was at the Beach. The other one was in Chesapeake. Ebony knew that he would not move too far and change Shawn's schooling. She figured that she would check them out when she went to Virginia in May for Diva's wedding.

Before that, she enlisted the help of Geno to help write a letter to the presiding judge over the case. A week later the information was forwarded back stating that the info would be held in a caption file. What the hell! This judge was not willing to work with Ebony at all. Shawn's future was at stake here. This wasn't about the parents, but the child was missing out on having a mother in his life.

Ebony's next step was filing a "Show Cause" motion. Lawrence hadn't upheld to the order. He never did. He only used the order to his advantage when Ebony needed or wanted more time with Shawn. Ain't this a bitch! It's a shame that the children suffer because of one of the parent's selfishness.

Everything was like it was gridlocked. Everywhere Ebony turned, she was being beaten up by life's problems. The only one she could really depend on now was Leroy. He knew how to make her smile, which was daddy's love! In all actuality, the pain was still there in her heart from her biological father.

Things began to take a turn for the worst. Leroy fell up the steps at his home and broke his arm. The doctors put a metal rod in it. Ebony went to visit him at the nursing home. Ebony didn't like the fact that her dad was there. For some reason rehabilitation centers and hospitals gave her the creeps. The smell of death lurked in the atmosphere.

In the back of her mind, she had already lost one parent. What would she do without her other one? Only time would tell. She tried to be strong for the both of them. Leroy had always been her rock in times of trouble, now she needed to be there for him. His hand had swollen up and looked like a boxing glove. He was in good spirits though, which made Ebony's eyes sparkle.

Everyday without fail, she would call him to lift up his spirits and hers for that matter. Leroy didn't know how long he was going to be there, but really wanted to go home. If he was going to meet his maker, he wanted it to be at his own residence. Ebony tried to take it one step further and call to see if she could bring Maxie (her dog). This always put a smile on his face.

Maxie could sense that something was not right the moment as he was carried into the facility. He began to shake uncontrollably. Three years had gone by and Vanessa didn't come around anymore, now Leroy was making his visits to Maxie even less. They say that dogs can sense things too.

Once the two entered the room, Leroy's face lit up and Maxie began to wag his tail. This made Ebony smile.

For Diva's wedding, Ebony brought along her close friend Malcolm. It wasn't like he was a stranger to Diva; he had met her a few years ago when Ebony had a cookout at the house. He didn't have a problem going. This would be there first out of town adventure together.

Malcolm was around 5'6" or 5'7" in height. A caramel mocha brother that was shorter than she like, but who cared. The two of them met back in 04', when Ebony had started working for the government. Ebony was bold and approached him. She learned to go after what she wanted. All he could do was turn her down. She took the chance!

Malcolm worked for the MTA as a police officer. He had been there for years. He was a lil older than Ebony, but she didn't care. She gave him the number and at no time did he reject it.

On their first date, Malcolm met Ebony at the Belvedere Hotel. They were going to the thirteenth floor for dinner and drinks. Dinner was very romantic, with candle lights and soft music. The two conversed to get to know one another more. After dinner, the two planned on going to the movies. Somehow things got mixed up and Ebony was waiting for what seemed like forever on her date.

Malcolm finally showed up stating that he had caught a flat tire on the way. The mood became a somber one and the two said goodnight without attending the movie. Nothing ever happened and when they crossed each other at work, the two just spoke.

The two always kept in touch and when she had to move out her first apartment, Malcolm came to her rescue. Ebony was glad that she had a man like that to have her back. The following year, once she finally purchased a home; Malcolm was there to pick up the slack again. Somehow this man seemed to always be there.

Wedding time and the search to find Shawn! As they arrived in the beach, the two got settled into the hotel. It wasn't real late, probably around nine o'clock in the evening. Ebony had told Malcolm what she planned on doing. She was glad that he was there with her. Ebony didn't know what would have happened if she found her child and her ex-husband would try to fight her.

The two set out to locate the address, it didn't take them long to find. The apartment complex didn't look too bad. Malcolm followed Ebony up the stairs. As the two approached the building, you could tell that the groundkeeper didn't do a good job. There were cobwebs in the corners of the apartment doors. Once they found the right apartment number, Ebony knocked on the door. She could hear the television on, but no one was answering the door. The two stood for about two minutes and no one even answered. Malcolm suggested that they try again before leaving town.

While hitting Wal-Mart, Ebony shown Malcolm all the damage her stupid ex had done to the property she had once owned, which was around the corner. As Ebony approached the property, it looked really nice. Malcolm could not believe his eyes.

"Yup, this was a nice house. To think that he destroyed it trying to get back at me, a damn shame," she said. Making her way down the street and around the corner, Malcolm wanted her to go back. "This seems like a nice quiet neighborhood. I can't believe he did all that damage to that house. Shit, I should have purchased it myself and fixed it up. This could have been a nice vacation home for me."

Diva's wedding was awesome. Her new husband was a minister. Ebony was so proud that Diva's prayers had been answered. At least someone had joy and it couldn't have happened to a better person. The bride was glowing and the groom was crying. That's tears of joy though! Ebony even cried as Diva's husband sang to her during the ceremony. For Ebony, it was good to be in the presence of a sister girl that she adored.

The following day it was time to hit the road again. But before Ebony left out of town, she was determined to go back to that apartment again. The two packed their bags and off they went.

This time Ebony could really see her surroundings. The two walked up the stairs, and Malcolm knocked that time. Ebony just stood hidden in the corner. She knew if her face was in the peek hole, they would never answer the door. No one even said who is it?

The door slowly opened and to Ebony's surprise, Shawn was standing before her eyes. She hadn't seen him since the summer of her mother's passing. He had grown tremendously. Ebony stepped from the shadows as Shawn was wiping sleep from his eyes. Once he leaned up and saw his mother, he was in shock.

Ebony thought she was gonna cry. She had found her child. It had taken her six months, but she did it. Ebony asked Malcolm to lend her $20 to give to her son. Before they could embrace good and for Shawn to get the money; Lawrence came to the door and saw Ebony. He quickly slammed the door.

Malcolm was heated and said "let's go." A part of her wanted to wait, but Malcolm was a no nonsense kind of person. The two walked down the stairs back to the car. As they got into the car and Malcolm started it up, Shawn came downstairs. His father had put his clothes on and stood at the top of the steps. He probably was wondering how in the world did she find his trifling ass.

Ebony got out of the car and hugged her son tight. He had given her, his cell number and that was cool with her. Shawn had grown up so tall and he was handsome too! As she gripped her son to hug him one last time, Lawrence stood there with more venom than she had ever seen.

Shit, he was getting child support money and she didn't have a right to know where her child was. "It really wasn't cool when you didn't get money, but now that you put the white bitch in the middle, motherfucker, I have a right to know where you live."

Ebony couldn't wait to get home fast enough, to write this old white bittie again. Now that Ebony was armed with his address, he could answer for the damage that the judge asked him not to do to the house. Once she got home, she would do another "Show Cause" on that ass.

Chapter 7

Mother's Day weekend and Ebony was driving once again to visit another old friend, Gwen. She hadn't seen Gwen in about eight years at this point. Very seldom did they talk by phone, cause she was in college to become a nurse. Ebony knew what it was like to study and she didn't want to bother her. "The day you graduate, is the day that I will be there." Ebony held true to her word. Barbara was willing to ride down to North Carolina also.

Ebony drove to North Carolina and dropped Barbara off at a church sister's house. She forged on to make it to Jacksonville which was about two more hours from where her grandmother was staying. Somehow, she got more lost then she had expected and was hided back to Virginia. Ebony was getting tired and knew this wasn't the way. Her power was dying on her phone and she was deep in redneck territory.

Once she got Gwen on the line and was told about the new roads that had mixed Ebony up, she was flying like a bat out of hell back down the highway. Gwen told her to be careful because of the deer, but Ebony didn't give a fuck. She was tired, sleepy and wanted to see her girl. By this time, she had already missed the graduation and the cookout.

Wouldn't you know it? A fucking DUI pitstop! What the hell? "I am too close now." The officer pulled Ebony over because she had Maryland plates. "License and registration, please, while shining the flashlight in Ebony's face. Ma'am where are you coming from?" "Sir, I have been driving all day trying to get to my girlfriend's graduation. I came from Baltimore and got lost. She said she was going to meet me at a Perry's convenient store in Jacksonville." "Ma'am, that is down the road. Drive safely and enjoy your stay." *Weew!*

Girl couldn't get their fast enough. Just to see her sister girl made it all worthwhile. Once they arrived at Gwen's home, Ebony had catching up to do. The girls sat on the patio and drank wine and chatted for what seemed like eternity.

The following day, Gwen showed Ebony around. They went to a strawberry farm and then to the mall. Ebony had to get Gwen something special for her graduation present.

Beauty counter, Dillard's here we come. Anything that the salesperson tried on Gwen, Ebony purchased.

Gwen had graduated with honors. Ebony was very proud of Gwen's accomplishments. Ebony reminisced on how she had met her and Gwen's self-esteem was shot to pieces. Gwen was Ebony's project back then; trying to escape from her own reality while with Lawrence. Now the two had both got out of their abusive relationships and did what their ex-spouses tried to hinder them from doing, getting DEGREES.

"What a short ass visit, but at least I got to see my girl!" Gwen had planned on coming to the big city (Baltimore) she called it in the following month. Ebony couldn't wait to show her around when she got to Baltimore.

Ebony made her way back to get her grandmother. As she loaded the car, and the two got back on the road; the next stop was Matthews,

Virginia. This was Ebony's grandfather side of the family. She could stop off and visit his gravesite also. Before hitting the Virginia line, Ebony received a text message from Shawn. "Happy Mother's Day."

Ebony hadn't heard that in years. Wow! "Baby, I am in Virginia and have your great grandmother with me. Would you like us to stop by?" "Yes." This would be twice in two weeks that she was going to see her child. She was just ecstatic just thinking about it.

She put the petal to the metal and flew to see her son. Once arriving, she texted Shawn to come outside. While outside, she wanted to get some current pictures of him. Barbara began to take pictures of Shawn and Ebony and Ebony did the same. This was precious moments, til the grim reaper appeared.

Lawrence stood at the top of the stairs with his arms folded. He even mean-mugged grandma. Grandma use to be in his corner. Ebony thought back when he called Barbara, "Get Ebony, she is throwing my clothes out the front door." She had come to his rescue and now he gonna forget how the family catered to him back in the day. Pure asshole!!!!!

"Let's go!" The three did a group hug and Ebony was once again saddened. Before the two could even reach Hampton, Lawrence was texting Ebony. "Don't come to my house again unannounced." *I bet you, he didn't say that shit to my face. Fuck you! My son asked me to come, and that's what I did. Would do it all over again, if he asked me too!*

It didn't take long but Ebony was back in court again. Lawrence now had to answer for the charges. "What's important here, the money or your child?" Once again this old bitch let him get off scott-free. *"Fuck that! Both are important. He fucked up my house. Received $10,000 and I still haven't seen or spoken to my child. Last time I checked, I sent you his damn address."* Things were falling on deaf ears.

Lawrence had a chance to stop the judge's order to stop the child support payments. He just stood there and let her continue. At that point Ebony could see that this wasn't about Shawn, this was revenge. Revenge for leaving his ass.

Chapter 8

So much damn stress! One thing after a fucking another! Ebony had to find some kind of escape from reality! She began taking up the hobby of reading. Urban novels, was the new thing and she lived vicariously through them. Her motto was "Sex she wasn't getting any, money she didn't have and drugs she didn't do them!" After reading this particular book, "The Black Door" by the author Velvet, it took on a new meaning for her. She had been without a man for a while. Her urges of sexual pleasure dominated her soul. Ebony was horny as hell! Going thru the day to day usual of using the showerhead to stimulate herself, was really getting old.

She could remember many of times when Lawrence would kick open the bathroom door while she was using the showerhead. "You use that more than you fuck me," he would say. She remembered him telling her, he would rather get a whore cause she didn't talk back, well the showerhead didn't hit or talk shit either. It provided relief! He also would take the showerhead and hide it. This was her only source of stimulation. Ebony didn't have to worry about any of that shit anymore. A hard dick is what she really wanted.

She was in need of some male companionship, nothing serious. A male's touch is what she longed for; his cologne encamped in her nostrils. Being intertwined with his body illuminating off heat, feeling the beats of his heart in the heat of passion, is what she wanted. If only for one night!

This particular day she was in the basement of her home searching on the computer for adult websites. Maybe if she just looked at some pictures this would cool down the burning sensation between her legs. She ran across this site called "Fling." The pictures excited her!

Everyone always say you gotta take a chance at something. And since this wasn't going to be a serious relationship, "Why the hell not?" You got mail! Damn already she thought! She looked at this person's profile, but deemed he was too young. He was a hottie though! What on earth was he doing on this website as fine as he was? Ebony only had one answer, *the same damn thing you are, crazy girl!* Yes, she had been with Kim who was younger than her, but not this young. He was only twenty-two.

The two started to reply with messages. "Sweetie, I am probably old enough to be your mother. What could you possibly want with me?" His response was, "I only deal with older women!" Her first thought NOT! "Add yourself as my friend and I will keep you in mind," she said. "Not a problem."

Three days later, the tingling was setting her shit on fire. She had to cool it off. With AIDS in the world today, you had to be careful, for some reason this was a chance she was willing to take. Ebony practiced safe sex anyway and had only been in two relationships since her divorce. Any man had to wear a condom until they got into a monogamist relationship with her. That's just the way it was.

She forwarded Mr. Thundercat a message. "Didn't have a way to contact you, but felt like some company the other day!" "I wasn't busy at all!" He provided Ebony with his number. Ebony got up the nerve to dial the number. Granted this was a sex site, so everyone knew why they were there (to get some ass.) Looking was being cautious, but eventually you had to take some kind of action. She didn't need to do the whole world, but just one would work for her. And if he played his cards right, every time she got horny, he would be the man to call on.

"Good evening," she said. Ebony introduced herself and he did the same. His name was Maze. As the two chatted for a minute, Ebony cut straight to the chase. She wanted to get laid and in the worst kind of way. She explained to Maze that she had never done this kind of thing before. Maze made Ebony feel very comfortable on the phone. He asked her to pick out the hotel and find out the cost. Once she had that information, then she could text it to him.

The plan was to meet that night. If she didn't, she would never have the courage to do this type of shit again. Ebony searched the net at work to find a hotel that was close by her house. The meeting place was to be at the Ramada Inn. Three hours to go . . . . Would she back out?

Ebony began to get butterflies in the pit of her stomach. Her nerves were getting the best of her. She had never done anything crazy such as this before. First time for everything, oh well! It was only one person that would judge her in the end anyway, and it sure wasn't man.

Geno was Ebony's co-worker that she confided almost everything in. The two had met a couple of years back and clicked at first sight. She confided in him her secret of what she was attempting to do. Geno never judged her. He just told her to be safe and call with the information. She could do that! Ebony had to get there first.

At 10:30p.m., the cell phone buzzed with a text message "Are you sure you really want to do this before I make reservations?" "YES!"

An hour to go and she already said yes. Ebony couldn't back out now, or could she! She was never scared of anything but Lawrence's dumb ass. Now that the violent part was over, she wasn't even really thinking about danger, only excitement. Before long, her walls would hopefully be filled with a hard throbbing dick. It was now nearing 11:45p.m. and the phone buzzed again "Room 452." There was no turning back now. Ebony texted back, "See you around 12:30."

Once she left work, she darted home to take a shower. Prior to getting there, all she could think of was getting laid, but in the back of her mind she was apprehensive. Suppose this was a mass murder that she was about to see? Did he have other people there to jump or gang rape her? All these crazy but true thoughts crossed her mind. Too late, she was going to ride it out and take a chance.

Slowly she lathered up the Vicky Secret body wash all over her. Intimate thoughts ran thru her mind. It had been so long since she felt a man's touch. In a few minutes hopefully, she would have the real thing. Ebony gracefully lotioned her body with pear scent in every crack and crevice. She put on a button down snap dress for easy access with sexy lingerie underneath. As she slipped on her high heels, she grabbed the keys and was headed out the door.

Once out front of the hotel, Ebony placed a quick call to Geno. Do or die! The butterflies were hitting her left and right. She came too far to turn back now.

She always kept a straight razor in her titties, for whatever may occur. Better safe than fucked up! Ebony was trying to get herself mentally prepared if something jumped off. As she got off the elevator, she took a deep breath; walked up to the door and KNOCKED!

The door slowly opened and the most handsome man she ever laid eyes on was standing before her. Maze's pictures on the internet didn't do him any justice; he was finer in person. Her pussy was really throbbing then or maybe because of what was about to go down.

Maze was around 5'10 or 5'11. He had a light to medium skinned complexion. Not too dark, not too light. His body was toned and he had the cutest dimples she had ever seen. He had a babyface, but, the body was saying Man all the way. Maze reached out and hugged Ebony to her surprise. Ebony was nervous and tried to make small talk. This was her usual way to calm herself down. The two sat on the bed and had a drink to lighten up the mood. Ebony had asked him prior to getting there his choice of liquor. That was the least she could do, since he paid for the room.

Maze had asked for some Remy, so Ebony got a shorty, just in case he was a dud. She didn't drink anything. She was high on life not to mention, Ebony had to be cognizant, since this was her first time out the gate.

It hadn't even been twenty minutes and her body had just had enough and couldn't take it anymore. She unsnapped her dress. As she laid with her lingerie on across the bed, Maze touched her body and the chills went up her spine. He went to put the condom on, but Ebony needed more. She had come this far and wanted the whole nine yards. Her body needed to be orally pleased also. Maze gently licked each nipple and made his way down town. The touch of his tongue hitting her pleasure spot sent chills up and down her spine. She was pleasingly surprised by his oral skills. Maze licked slowly and gently on her clitoris as she grabbed his head and thrusted him deeper into her core of love. She held his head in place so long that he was begging for air.

It wasn't long before her body started to shake. Her legs were wrapped around his neck; everything she had bottled up inside of her was being released. She came as hard as hurricane Katrina in the Mississippi delta. It was a blessing he had a strong neck cause she didn't break it. This was pure insatiable bliss! Ebony's body was vibrant and on fire. It had been so long!

She grabbed the cup of ice and put some ice cubes in her mouth. Ebony gently moved up and down Maze's chest with the ice. As she moved further down, she engulfed his manhood in her mouth. Maze wasn't ready for all that she was giving him. His head fell back and he began to moan. The ice cubes was doing the trick, as she slowly licked and sucked up and down all of his eight inches. Ebony didn't want to make him cum just yet, so she teased him making him want more. She whispered in his ear, "I need you inside me."

Maze placed the condom on his tool and had his way with Ebony. The pleasure that was built up was now bubbling over! He had her body in every position imaginable. The pleasure he gave was well worth it. The two sexed for hours with limited intermissions. This was right up her alley. It had been so long and technically she didn't know if and when she would have sex again. She really didn't want Maze to stop, but he ran out of condoms.

Ebony offered to go to her car and get some more, but she had exhausted him. As she let the man come up for some air, the two began to chat awhile before she left. Around four thirty as she was getting ready to leave, she had one request for Maze: could she see him again! It was just that good!

The four minute trip home had Ebony in la-la land. Finally her walls had been filled to capacity and all the stress that was bottled up inside of her was now released. She thought to herself, this was well worth the chance taken! Maze was just a loveable person. Everyone had their reasons for being on a sex site, she knew she had hers, but damn! That was a workout. This young thundercat turned her world inside out. Mission accomplished!

Chapter 9

Time was flying and Leroy's health was beginning to deteriorate. Ebony would try to phone, but as of late, his wife was accepting all his calls. She couldn't stand Ebony with a passion. It wasn't Ebony's fault that her husband messed with Ebony's mother. Leroy had married this woman to take care of his children. Two months later, he had met Ebony's mother. If only he had waited.

Ebony couldn't be concerned with that at this point. Her main focus was to stick by her parent til the end. She knew that the cancer had spread through his body since the doctor's had placed the rod in his arm. Ebony began to grow weary because his conversations were limited now.

Knowing how they had been so close for thirty four years and especially since her mother had passed. The two were thick as thieves. Everything that the three of them did (casinos, shopping and dinner) was still done with the memory of Vanessa there with them. Now Ebony was facing things on her own.

For Ebony's birthday, she decided that she was going out of the country. The Dominican Republic sounded like a winner. She just needed time to get away and have some peace.

Things had been going well with Maze also. Ebony took a liking to this young man. It was something special that she wanted to make him, her little prince. No more spending money on a hotel, he could have the luxury of coming to her home. Maybe she was trying to break the initial rules, and play for keeps.

Everytime Maze would come over; Ebony turned up the excitement more and more. She knew in her heart that he was seeing other people. Did she think that she could settle him down? At one point, she even offered him a key to the crib. Wasn't like she was seeing other people, only him. It had been a year now and they weren't using protection either. If she caught something she knew where she got it from.

His birthday was five days before hers. She wished like hell he would go to the island with her, but he kept his distance with that. Maze just kept telling Ebony, "That would be nice."

Ain't nothing wrong with getting a little loving before you leave though!!! Ebony would rather take her chances here then to go out of the country and get something that her ass couldn't get rid of. At least she had a number and full name of Maze, and not an islander with no way to get in touch or to whop that ass either.

Maze came over and brought Ebony's birthday in with her before leaving for the airport. Ebony never got a chance to go to sleep before getting on the plane. The two fucked for hours. He was happy with his birthday gift (the awesome sex). Ebony couldn't have been more pleased her damn self. Each time they got together, there was the combustible chemistry that was off the hook. Ebony made sure that he learned something new and erotic.

Ebony could feel the attachment to this man. But did he feel the same way? Blinded by the lust of everything overpowering her, she blocked that part out. It was good to have a young man to knock her back out. Women her age would die for the same shit. Just to have someone cater to your needs, keeps a woman defenses down!

The trip was fun, but it was nothing like having a man to go with you. Ebony went with her cousin. They meet two nice couples there while on vacation. Everyone clicked right off the bat. Everyday, they ate breakfast, lunch and dinner together. Went to the casino and clubs and had plenty of laughs.

Something was getting ready to knock the breath out of her once again. Ebony thought about it while away, "Pop never called for my birthday. This is odd behavior." Once she returned back home, things weren't looking so good for Leroy.

Call it a premonition, but Ebony had been back about two weeks now. She really wasn't tired; but something was nagging her in her gut. As she crawled out of bed and entered the bathroom; she fell to her knees and began to pray.

Father in the name of Jesus, I thank you Lord. Please put your loving arms around my stepfather. Please show me a sign of why I am on this earth. My mother is gone. My real father doesn't care. My stepdad is dying and his wife won't let me talk to him. My ex-husband is keeping me away from my son. What is there left for me to do? I don't want to go on.

Tired and exhausted, the phone began to ring at seven fifteen. "Hello." Ebony could hear a voice on the other end, stating that the man that raised her was now gone. Ebony sat clean up in the bed and cried her ass off. Who was gonna take care of her now? Who was going to be her rock in the time of troubles?

Ebony tried to come to grips with the fact that both of her parents were now gone. Maybe the break that she had endured with not seeing Leroy was preparing her for this very moment.

Ebony began to reflect on her life. *Glad I made it back in time to spend with both of my parents. I don't think that I would never have been strong enough to handle these tragedies, if the both of them hadn't raised me to be the person that I am. All I could do is take away what they have taught me and try to instill it in Shawn. I hope I have made both of them proud.*

Ebony was sure going to miss her parents. She knew she would always hold them dear to her heart, but now **"GOD"** needed both of them more. *Hope the two of you are shopping, dancing and still loving one another up there. Please look after me from up above. I love you both.*

Once seeing Leroy laying in the casket, Ebony took it harder than she had when her mother passed. Ebony always looked up to her stepfather. He may have not been her biological one, but Leroy was more than her biological one could have ever been to her.

Ebony was even madder at his wife. She tried to exclude Ebony out of everything. Vanessa and Ebony knew more about Leroy then his wife and his own children did. Ebony called all his friends to break the news. His friends thought that Vanessa was his wife. Every function he went to, Vanessa and Ebony were there. They barely knew his real wife.

"Look at this simple bitch? Like she knew all these people. My dad had plenty of friends and clubs that he was into, that you could have cared less. Now you sitting there acting like you were the loving wife." Ebony had to regain her composure. She remembered her dad telling her, "I am not leaving nothing to anyone. I have enough insurance to get buried and that's it. If you didn't get it while I was alive, you won't receive."

He had given plenty to Vanessa and Ebony over the course of thirty four years. Ebony couldn't complain. She was hurt when his sister said that her dad's wife had cleaned his room out like he never lived in the house before he was even in the ground. All she wanted was his house that he and his first wife had. Golddigger!

Chapter 10

The problem with men started because Ebony had always been trying to get the love and affection from RL, her father. Ever since she was a child there was nothing anyone could say about the man, that she wouldn't take offense too. Vanessa never talked bad about him. Guess she figured that Ebony would grow up and find out for herself. As Ebony was told, early on in life RL was there for her financially. RL's life took a turn when he first went to prison when Ebony was four. That is when Vanessa discovered that he was on drugs, his attitude became unbearable. That didn't stop Ebony from loving him. She just wished that when he was home from prison, he spent quality time with her. It was if he stepped aside and let Leroy raise his child.

All the years of trying to be daddy's girl, searching for a man in her life that could fill the void she was missing. Often times she used sex as a tool to be with these men, but the bottom line was her needing her father's love. All the years of trying to connect with him were in vain. Ebony's most treasurable moments should have been happy, but they were filled with pain. Deep down Ebony didn't think that RL cared about the way she felt anyway.

As Ebony began to relive her childhood, "My sixth grade graduation, looking the entire ceremony for him to not show. Strike one . . . Afterwards, she had walked about twelve blocks to his home to find him nodded out in the chair. Was that more important than your child? Senior prom, RL did surprise me though and showed up at the house. Oh, but that time, he was running from the Po-Po. Did that count? Senior graduation rolled around and he made every excuse in the book not to go. "I don't have clothes and I don't want to walk with these canes" he said. The reason he was walking with canes in the first place was because he got shot in a drug house. Aunt Ally had called that dreadful morning before school to break the news.

RL was still her father and Ebony was taught to honor her parents. As she had visited him in the hospital, they didn't think he was going to make it. Ebony broke down and cried. As RL came too, "Don't cry. Tony the Tiger just got hurt this time. I am going to be alright," he said. True to form, Ebony didn't think he would recover from being paralyzed; but he did it. She went as far as catching buses after school to rehab to take him food and spend time with him.

The big day; her wedding when she asked him to help walk her down the aisle. He got nervous and wouldn't. It was always Leroy right by her side. Ebony loved Leroy as her dad, but still she wanted and needed RL in her life."

As the years passed, she still longed for his love. Even after returning home from leaving Lawrence, Ebony found RL at his mother's house. He had been staying there. What did she have to do to make her own father show her some love? She made it a point to reach out to him. Ebony had invited him for breakfast with her and Leroy. Even Leroy had agreed to pick RL up. Right before the pickup, he would cancel. Ebony had to admit this still hurt. Even when her mother passed, he called Leroy not her.

Ebony still tried to reach out and let him know that she bought a house. "Why the fuck you buy a house? Your mother's house is yours."

Ebony fought back, "What do you have to leave me, nothing? I don't even know where you live. I didn't call you to be cursed out. I thought that you would be happy for me."

A couple of years later, RL had heard that Leroy was sick and reached out to Ebony. Never once did he say hello, he just started in about her stepdad being sick. Ebony was tired of his shit too! "Excuse me! Hello, how are you? Do you know what day it is?" It was Vanessa's birthday and Ebony was making her way to the cemetery. This sort of hurt her. How could he be so insensitive?

The day of Leroy's funeral, RL showed up smelling like liquor. He hadn't seen Ebony since Vanessa's funeral. Inside the vestibule of the church, RL screamed "Why you got on all that makeup?" This was not the time or the place for that. Ebony had just lost her dad and she was fighting mad. "Do you know what I suppose to look like? Just know that I look like you." Barbara told Ebony that she must honor thy mother and thy father. "My mother is no longer here and don't you see my father laying in the casket in there."

For the life of her, she didn't know what was wrong with her biological father. She looked just like him. "Why deny me the love?" Couldn't he see that Ebony had been carrying this pain inside for years? Everytime Ebony wanted to tell him how she truly felt, he would say, "If you called for this shit, I don't want to hear that fucking shit." Ebony would just cry.

Remembering what Vanessa told her, tell him how you feel. If he chooses to come around fine; if not fine. Do you part and then leave it alone. Guess Ebony would have to leave it alone and close that chapter of her life.

Chapter 11

2010, the big 4-0 was rolling around! Come hit one of these islands with me girls!!!!

She asked a couple of friends, but everyone said their money was a little tight. Shit! So was Ebony's, but she was getting the hell out of B-More. Also; one of her girlfriend's husband had some dumb shit to say about the situation. "What ya'll going to get ya'll groove back, like Stella?" Ebony just wanted this trip to be drama free. That cancelled her girlfriends. Since everyone had jumped ship and couldn't go, Ebony turned to Malcolm.

There was no question in his mind when Ebony asked about going away, he jumped at the chance and said "Yes." Their friendship had grown to the point that she became his ride or die chick. After traveling to Diva's wedding last year, they had learned more about one another. Malcolm opened up a little about himself, but you could tell he was holding back something. He was still a mystery.

Ebony had trouble seeing that this man was always there for her. When her back was up against the wall, Malcolm always came to her rescue. At times just so she wouldn't be by herself, she would call him and take him out. She figured that was the least she could do for all the times he had come through when she most needed it.

There was never a time when Malcolm ever asked Ebony for sex. This was unusual in her eyesight. Every man she knew always wanted to fuck, if they helped out. Not Malcolm, he was in a class of his own.

It finally dawned on Ebony that just maybe her best friend had been the one for her all the time. She would dare not try and cross the line. But this game the two of them was playing with each other had to stop somewhere. "While in Cancun, I am going to make the first move, all he can do is reject me," she thought.

The phone rang at 10:00 am, the following morning. Who in the hell could this be? "Hello" in her irritated voice! Malcolm was on the other end. "I know you don't get up til one, but tomorrow be ready to go to the travel agency."

Ebony arose early to meet Malcolm. While waiting for her agent to come in, the two looked around. Kathy soon arrived and the three began to talk about resorts. Ebony already knew which resort she wanted to go to, The Dreams Mexico. If it was anything like The Dreams in Punta Cana, she would enjoy it. Malcolm let her choose anyway, because it was going to be her birthday. Deep in her heart, she wanted this trip to be special. She saw something special in this man.

Kathy booked the trip and placed them in an ocean front room with a king bed. Ebony spoke up and was like "Didn't you book us for two double beds!" "No, I think you and your man will have a good time!" Kathy stated. Ebony explained that Malcolm was not her man, that he was just a friend. Kathy had that sparkle in her eye. Ya'll make a great couple. Malcolm jokingly stated, "I will put her on the floor!" They all laughed. The two were used to traveling and not touching each other anyway.

Ebony and Kathy was surprised when Malcolm had paid for the whole trip in full. Ebony was use to making payments for her vacations. This came as a shock. Since they were going as friends, Ebony would pay for her share. It only took her a week to pay for her portion in full to Malcolm.

The year had been spinning so fast, it seemed like every month Malcolm and Ebony had planned something together. Out of the blue, Ebony received a call asking to attend a Mary Mary concert. She never turned him down. Deep in her heart, she knew he was the one for her. His tough exterior often times weakened her. Ebony became powerless around him. Her outspokenness had all but ceased. She wanted to know what he was hiding under that tough exterior! Time would tell . . . .

Malcolm picked her up sharply at 6pm. The two really didn't call these dates, but technically they were. Although they both were dressed casually with jeans and nice shirts, one would have thought otherwise.

Ebony never saw Malcolm as the big brother type. Before the concert, the two ate at Ram's Head in Annapolis. The concert had an intimate setting, not like the usual big crowd. Ebony really enjoyed herself. Just being around Malcolm made her a little weak.

The both of them had been through traumatic relationships before. It probably was best that they had been friends for so long. Ebony always felt comfortable with an older man. Malcolm sort of reminded Ebony of her stepfather.

Chapter 12

Sparks were coming! Ebony didn't know if it was good or bad, but she was hoping for the absolute best to come her way. In spite of all that she had been through over the years, it was time for something better to happen. Their phone conversations went from once every month gradually to about three to four times a month.

Ebony was at work surfing the web, when Hampton Jazz fest flashed on one of her emails. Like clockwork, the first person she dialed was Malcolm. Ebony hadn't been there since her mother and stepfather were living. Technically she really enjoyed going to concerts. It had been long enough and this would be a change. Also she could pick up Shawn after the show. Once again, not turning her down, it was a date.

As the days were approaching for the first day of ticket sales, Malcolm called. "I have tried to get on my computer to order them, but the computer is acting crazy." He asked Ebony to get a pen and paper. He provided her with his credit card information, and the girl was shocked. She thought that he would at least ask to use her computer to order them. All she could think, "I must be real trustworthy for him to do that. Both of us need to stop playing around and do the damn thing."

By them still not being a couple, Ebony felt like she needed to do her part also. She purchased the hotel room for the three day event. Remembering what her mother always told her, pay your own way, and that's what she did.

Two months before the show . . . .

Ebony had been trying to contact Shawn but to no avail. Every time she did get through and ask about report cards or grades, the story was "He's fine!" This particular time, Lawrence emailed that Shawn was failing a couple of classes. "Have him call me." To her surprise, he let her son call her that evening. As she chatted with her son, it was like he was a zombie over the phone. Granted, she had heard him speak like this before; only stating yes and no, but something didn't sit right this particular time. Lawrence had dominated him and he was restricted to what he could say to his mother.

Ebony let her son know that she was very disappointed in his grades and that he would not be able to come to Baltimore for the summer. She urged Lawrence to find summer schooling for their child. Ebony suggested that Shawn be enrolled in Sylvan Learning Center and a counselor. Shawn was in serious need of help. It was like only Ebony could see that. Lawrence was non-chalant about the situation. "Shawn is not stupid; he just wants to be a clown. He is a typical teenager. You don't know him like I do." "Duh! You never let him talk or see me unless you are trying to get rid of him. How the fuck are we supposed to bond, when you block our relationship?" These statements made it clear that it wasn't about what was best for Shawn, but the child support.

Ebony was fuming. "Shawn gonna turn out just like his dad, if I don't find a way to prevent it." She had just had enough of Lawrence trying to play the mother role. The court system had fucked her royally with no grease! Granted most women did this to men, but she didn't deserve what she was getting. It was like she couldn't even have input on how her child was being raised. She was being used as a financial donor only. To avoid the pain, Ebony constantly tried to block it out of her mind. Deep in her heart every time she did this, the pain worsened. Shawn needed better in his life, but the court system wasn't trying to help Ebony or her child for that matter. The bottom line was that Lawrence was still getting what he wanted "Control!" No help would be in the foreseeable future until Shawn was of age and Ebony no longer had to deal with Lawrence. The day was coming, three more years to go!

June was here! Shawn's 15th birthday! She hadn't heard from him since April about the school work. Ebony tried to reach him by phone at least three times. She found it odd and practically strange that he would not pick up the phone for his big day. Two days earlier she had sent Shawn a card. Ebony knew he should have gotten it by now. She remembered him telling her that his father took all his money from him during his last visit, so she sent him none. Shawn knew that Ebony would give him whatever he wanted when he was in her presence. After not hearing from him on his birthday, she knew Lawrence was behind it.

Ebony emailed Lawrence once again to get Shawn for the summer. Granted she went back on her word, but what more could she do? Something in her gut told her things with Shawn was not good. She had to get to him and find out the problem. Call her crazy, but mother's intuition kicked in.

The date was confirmed to pick up Shawn for when Ebony and Malcolm would be in Virginia. She didn't like being in the presence of Lawrence by herself. His stare of hatred towards Ebony gave her weird vibes. She always had someone with her, and lately it had been Malcolm. This made Lawrence even madder!

Arriving in Virginia for the Hampton Jazz fest was a much needed getaway. Malcolm had a lot of things on his mind, but being in the company of Ebony eased a little of what he was going through. Ebony never questioned what was going on; she figured he would open up if he wanted to.

The two, first stopped off at Diva's house for some good ole` fried chicken. During dinner, Diva's husband, asked Malcolm were they a couple. This was the second time someone asked that same damn question! Malcolm's response was "No!" After about an hour of fellowship, Diva was leaving for her high school reunion in New York and Ebony had to check into the hotel to get ready for the show that was going to start in an hour. Malcolm and Ebony hated to eat and run.

The two ladies embraced one another and Ebony looked at Diva and asked her to pray for her and Malcolm. Everyone could see that they were good together. Ebony was starting to open her eyes and believe it herself. The only person needed to realize it now, was Malcolm.

The two had an awesome time at the show. Gladys Knight was the headliner for Friday's show. She put it down. Ebony danced and sang during the whole show. Driving back to the room she was exhausted. She had been running all morning then driving, getting stuck in traffic in Virginia and the concert. Malcolm had been playing cards all night the night before, so he was no help to her in driving there. Her body was drained and she knew he was an early riser. No rest for the weary! After arriving back to the room, they took their separate showers and turned into bed. Ebony said goodnight and turned her back and went to sleep, that's how tired she was. She was now used to traveling with Malcolm and nothing sexual ever happening, this night would be no different. The only thing that she didn't like was that he woke up too damn early for her. He always wanted to go eat breakfast.

Chapter 13

Morning came and Ebony was asleep when Malcolm eased up behind her. She opened one eye to see what time it was. She really didn't want to move yet. He began to rub her back. Malcolm's hands moved up her night gown and Ebony was shocked. All she could think of was "Don't breathe girl! Don't even think about making a move, if you do he will probably stop. Let's see where this little adventure is going."

Malcolm gently fondled her breasts and made a gesture that she turn to face him. Once facing him in a half sleepy daze, he pulled her nightgown up and softly caressed and kissed her plump nipples. Ebony had all sort of things running through her mind. It had been six years of knowing him and now FINALLY! As he licked each nipple, Ebony's legs began to spread apart. Malcolm took his time and ventured down to her love opening. As he began to lick and suck on her clit, Ebony's head just fell back and she was in ecstasy. She had waited a long time for that very moment and didn't want it to end. The pressure had mounted up from this being their first encounter that she released all of her juices. It didn't take Malcolm long to just get up and go in the bathroom.

Damn, it's over! Ebony wasn't going out like that. She had waited for far too long and didn't want the moment to be over. Did he regret what he had just done and had to rethink the situation? He finally exited the bathroom and before he could approach his side of the bed, girlfriend was down on her knees to return the favor. Ebony reached for his manhood. As she gently touched it, she began to kiss and caress it. Within a few strokes, and her trying to get into her groove, he had already released his fluids with the quickness. It must have been a long time for him also. This long awaited moment flew by too quick.

The two got themselves together and got dressed. As she drove for breakfast, the two were silent. Once reaching their destination, the two still didn't have much to say to one another. The tension was so thick you could cut it with a knife. Ebony tried her hardest to make small talk. When the attempts failed, she kept rewinding in her mind what she should have done differently.

Once breakfast was over, they once again ventured around Virginia Beach. By this time, Malcolm loosened up when she began telling him the sites. The time was slipping away. They wanted to try and get a nap before dinner and the show that evening. Ebony had already seen Diva but hadn't let Deja know that she was in town yet. Ebony placed a text to Deja informing her of the address of the hotel. She hadn't seen Deja in some years, but the two always texted or called one another. As the two made their way back to the hotel, Ebony got a call that Deja was on her way to visit. This gave Malcolm time to take a nap.

Before Ebony could lay down good, the phone rang and Deja was waiting in the lobby of the Westin. Once Ebony departed from the elevator, it was if their relationship never missed a beat. The girls were so happy to see each other. It had been about seven years. They had so much to catch up on. As they sat in the lobby, Deja began to give her the 411 on how things in VA were going. Deja's children were growing up really well. The oldest had already graduated school and had started attending college. The middle child was an honor roll student and the youngest was smart as a whip also. Ebony was so proud. She had been truly grateful to Deja for the all the nights she had slept on her floor. It was nothing but a tremendous blessing to have true friends. Ebony never forgot when she first moved back home either. She was indebted to this woman. Ebony asked about group meetings that they used to attend and the people both of them had in common. The two chatted away as if it were yesterday that they had spoken to one another.

Look at the time! Before they knew it, two hours had escaped them. Deja had been working hard trying to make ends meet. Ebony remembered during their conversation that Deja's cell phone wasn't working properly. This would be the perfect time to give back. Ebony explained to Deja to expect a package the following week. She was now in a position to return the blessings. Ebony was really getting tired, but had no time for a nap. The girls said their goodbyes and promised to talk via the phone next week once the package arrived. It was time to wake up Malcolm.

Once again no sleep for Ebony, but it was well worth it to catch up with an old friend. Malcolm and Ebony got back on the road for dinner before the show. Ebony wanted to take Malcolm to the famous Captain George's in the Beach. She broke the silence with the lineup for that particular night. Tonight *Teena Marie and Charlie Wilson*, Ebony thought. Sitting at the table Ebony told Malcolm that she put her money on Lady T. Ebony knew this Blue Eyed Sista of Soul was gonna tear the house down. Charlie may have been the headliner, but Ebony had seen Teena before. Standing ovation! Malcolm chose Charlie and it was a bet. Ebony enjoyed dinner but it seemed like they were always rushing. It was time to get back to the hotel, shower and change for the concert. Just an hour and a half, til they found out who would win. Traffic was always horrendous crossing the Hampton Road Bridge Tunnel. The two rushed and got dressed and off they went.

Ebony could only focus on tonight; she was gonna test those waters. He had started something, so she was going to finish it. She wasn't done with his ass yet! He just teased her with that sampler. Good thing she did pack a chemise like Geno told her to do. Normally she was strapped with her regular pj's when traveling with Malcolm. This would give her a good excuse to use it tonight, since he had taken her on this endeavor.

Ebony knew that she had won the bet on the show, if only they had wagered some money. The game plan was to put the damn thing down on him once they had taken their showers. After getting back to the room, Malcolm took his shower first. Ebony took her sweet lil time in the bathroom. She was trying to get up the courage to unfold this deck of cards she was getting ready to play. Gamblers must know when to hold them and when to fold them. Kenny Rogers stated it best.

Now the ball was in Ebony's court! As she exited the bathroom door, she was smelling so good from lotioning every ounce of her body. She had the sexy chemise on. Malcolm was sitting up in the bed watching tv or pretending to anyway. Ebony eased onto the bed, and began to kiss his neck. He never moved, like there was no emotion at all. She made her way downtown, but that didn't seem to faze him either. Ebony didn't know what to think at this point. It had been months since she last been with Maze, so she wasn't getting any sex. Fuck it! She just finally straddled him, but that was short lived. Ebony couldn't even get her cowboy ride on good, before it was over. Damn, Damn, Damn, in her Florida Evans voice!!! That really didn't matter to her though! It was more of an emotional connection with Malcolm. In the words of Tamar Braxton, that was a hotmess.com.

Ebony thought back on all the years as friends and how he never approached her in a sexual manner. She really didn't care if the encounter didn't last long. The fact of the matter was that he didn't refuse her advance. Her body for the most part was thrilled and satisfied, that she immediately drifted off to sleep.

The next morning things were a little better. This day Malcolm let her sleep. Before the bright morning sun could hit her eyes, she was awaken with coffee and muffins for breakfast in bed. Maybe what had transpired did light a spark under him. Malcolm explained to her that he just couldn't sleep and had walked around the hotel looking at sites since five in the morning. He also had gone to the gym and the pool before wanting to wake Ebony.

Chapter 14

The final day of their little mini vacation was coming to a close. Ebony wanted to enjoy it til it was over. She didn't know where this was going to lead, but she was down for the ride. As she got out of bed to start packing her clothes for checkout, she called Shawn and Lawrence's phones. No answer! He knew she was coming, how slick of him. Once Malcolm and Ebony got dressed, Ebony decided that they should just go to Lawrence's apartment. He only lived a couple of blocks from the hotel.

Once at Lawrence's house, Malcolm stayed in the car. As Ebony approached the door and knocked, Lawrence answered in a half sleepy daze. She explained that she had tried to call both phones with no such luck. Lawrence's demeanor was a little awkward. He always held much hostility when talking to Ebony and always kept a tight leash on Shawn. This particular day for some reason he was in a hurry to get rid of Shawn. Lawrence stated that Shawn's clothes were already packed and at the door. Ebony could take Shawn now. This was unusual, no fight! Something was behind this. As Ebony thought about it, this fucker must have a new woman. Ebony politely busted his bubble. He would have to wait a little while longer so he could be free and clear of Shawn. Ebony clarified that she couldn't, that she had plans and that Lawrence should meet her in Hampton when she called. She also stated that she could put her son's suitcase in the car to assure him that she was serious.

Before arriving to the concert, Malcolm and Ebony stopped off to the Golden Corral once again. As the two sat down and prepared to eat, they mostly talked about Shawn. Malcolm was always excited to see Shawn. He thought that Ebony had a fine well-mannered son.

Once the two got to the Coliseum, Ebony was surprised. Malcolm began to hold her hand like they were a couple. The game was beginning to change or was it? The show was running behind schedule so Ebony texted Shawn to let him know that when the concert was over or close to it, she would text both Lawrence and Shawn. Shawn was elated. For the first time in a while, he got to communicate with his mother.

Lawrence began to really pressure Ebony about getting Shawn before five o'clock. Why was he in a rush? If the two had to meet at Kings Dominion like the court order stated at five, he couldn't have gotten there and back for his plans before then. She was being kind enough to pick Shawn up in Hampton so that Lawrence wouldn't have to drive that far. Sometimes you just can't be nice to a nigga at all. During the intermission, Ebony placed a call to Lawrence to find out what was really going on. "I won't have my car after five o'clock." He stated. Ebony once again could not believe that he chose a woman over his child. How the fuck you gonna lend your vehicle to someone knowing that you have to send your child off? The tension began to rise and Ebony discussed it with Malcolm. Malcolm didn't understand Lawrence's behavior but wanted to make sure Ebony didn't stress. "We can pick him up after the show. He is just being difficult as usual," he said. This took some of the pressure off of her. Malcolm was like her sounding board.

Frankie Beverly was up next and Ebony was ecstatic. She had claimed this man as *her baby daddy* for years. Only in her mind, but she liked living in fantasy world sometimes. Their plane had just landed, so that was the holdup for the show. Ebony didn't care and the whole crowd didn't mind the delay either. During the initial start, Frankie's voice was hoarse. This really didn't tend to matter, the crowd took over. Yes, they sang all the songs for him. They jammed and he still got a standing ovation. Ebony began to think "This man hasn't made a record in over twenty years and can still move the crowd." It was now 7 p.m. and the show was finally over. Ebony conceded and was returning back to pick up Shawn.

During the course of the twenty minute ride that turned into two hours, Ebony was boiling at this point. That fucker (Lawrence) could have met her in Hampton. She bitched the entire time riding to his apartment. Ebony only calmed down after Malcolm told her to look at the bright side, she was getting her child. He felt as though Shawn belonged with Ebony anyway. After making that trip again for the second time that day, Ebony was getting ready to go knock on the door. "I don't want you to go upstairs. I can't see you and I don't want to have to fuck your ex-husband up."

Ebony kindly placed a call for Shawn to come downstairs. The motherfucker walked Shawn downstairs and had the nerve to come with an attitude. He had his nerve after the fucked up situation he had placed her in. Shawn was smiling and never even acknowledged bye to his dad.

Malcolm got out of the car and Ebony crossed over into the passenger seat, Lawrence stood there with venom in his eyes. Malcolm didn't flinch. He wanted Lawrence to step to him, so that he could bust that ass for everything he had ever heard about the man.

The three pulled off and Ebony stated to Shawn, "I know that I punished you from coming to Baltimore this summer, but I had a feeling something wasn't right when I called for your birthday and you didn't answer." Shawn replied, "You must have been reading my mind." Ebony needed her son to elaborate further, but would wait until he opened up. Damn, the traffic was once again thick on the return trip home. Four hours now of just sitting at the bridge, this didn't make any sense. This so-called father or wanna be mother, Lawrence was playing, only cared about who he could control. He was still pulling the strings and getting everything his way. Not this time because Ebony rode to Baltimore with her precious son and her possible future husband or at least her new man.

Chapter 15

"Mom, for my birthday when I received the card, Daddy was standing over me waiting to see if I got money. He was like, "she ain't send you no money?" I just smirked at him. I am not allowed to call you or answer any of your calls. Daddy told me that I can't answer for any of my family that is on your side. Everytime I come home he checks my phone to make sure. He always asking me questions about who Mr. Malcolm is to you? Do you live in a house or apartment? I just tell him that Mr. Malcolm is a good friend and yes she does live in a house. I don't know why he asks me all these questions!"

"Why the fuck he want 411 on me? I don't call about whatever trick he got!" *My focus is my child and why bagger him with questions? This nigga is obsessed in trying to make me miserable.*

Just listening to this foolishness was making Ebony sick. *And yet this motherfucker claimed he loved me! He never bothered his first wife or this last one, why me? This shit ain't love, it is an obsession he has with me. The only thing that still glues us together is Shawn. He is making this child suffer to get back at me. The child shouldn't be caught in the middle of this. Someone please help me and give me strength!*

Shaking her head, Ebony just changed the subject with her child. Vanessa never talked bad about RL, and Ebony sure wasn't going to do it with her son. When he got old enough, he could see the evil that his father did during the years.

"Shawn, baby, we need to be on the two year plan. If it means boot camp for you, then that's what it gotta be. Do not disrespect your father. Do your studies and when you turn eighteen, you don't have to live with me; but you damn sure ain't gotta stay there." Ebony spat to her child.

Since Shawn had been there, Malcolm would come over while Shawn was with family. He had a key ever since Leroy had taken ill. Malcolm lived close by and he was the quickest to get to her in the time of need. "I am on my way, but oh I forgot, I have a key." Ebony just smiled.

Riding up the highway Ebony had explained that she was tired of going around the block; she wanted to go for a long ride. She had to speak in code, because her child was in the back seat. In other words, she was really ready to give her heart and soul to someone.

Malcolm totally agreed. When he came over, he sat down and had a long talk with Ebony. He tried to analyze her life to see what makes her tick. Ebony didn't pick that up. She thought he was just listening to her view points. He looked into her eyes, and told her that he didn't play games. "When I love, I love for real," he said. He passionately kissed Ebony and for once in her life, she was receptive to it.

The two began to fool around only when Shawn was away for the weekend. Ebony was beginning to tear down the blocks one by one, that had been built up around her. She had blocked everyone that came in her world out since Lawrence. She was finally ready to explore love and not lust, this time around. This girl was scared to go through the same thing over again.

Ebony needed time to herself to grow as a person and really get to love herself before she could love someone else. It had taken her seven years to do it, but now she was definitely ready.

The chemistry was off the hook. Ebony never knew what intimacy was til now. How could a man be so passionate and get inside her head?

This man had her cumming without oral stimulation or penetration. This had never happened in her life. Just the sweetest touch of him blew her mind.

The times that Shawn was home, Ebony was excluded from dinner. It was just him and Malcolm. Malcolm would pick him up and they would go to Stone Cold Creamery. Malcolm wanted to learn more about Shawn also. This was a package deal. Take it or leave it.

The weekend before taking Shawn home, Malcolm and Ebony discussed taking Shawn to K.D. to the park before returning him to his father. Malcolm became excited, because he hadn't rode on a rollercoaster in years. Getting pumped by the situation, Ebony really thought that this was now a family unit. She wasn't ready to let Shawn know yet, but Ebony had a glow that you couldn't wipe off her face.

Ring, Ring! "Hello," "I know you sleep, but can you check in Shawn's room and see if my son's I-POD is in there," Miko, her cousin said. Ebony got up and started looking around. She never seen Shawn with an I-POD. Miko began to explain how much it costed, and that the last person seen with it was Shawn. Ebony didn't have money like that. As she took one final look, nothing. Something told her to check in the nightstand drawer, bingo.

Miko's husband must have flown Shawn home on a jet, he got there just that quick before Ebony and Miko could hang up. Shawn gave him the $50 that Malcolm had given him earlier. Ebony was really disappointed in this kind of behavior. Miko was her backup plan, and he spoiled that. "Don't you realize she has been buying you tennis shoes whenever you come here? She takes care of you and feed you while I am at work, since Mommie is gone. Why would you steal from them or anyone for that matter? Didn't you know better?" Shawn had no excuse for his actions. He saw that his mother was hurt and just cried.

Ebony got on the horn and apologized to Miko. She also tried calling Lawrence but no answer. Her final call was to Malcolm. Malcolm couldn't believe what he was hearing. He stepped up to the plate and talked to Shawn, like his father should have if Ebony could ever get him to contact her.

Three days later after numerous attempts, Lawrence finally answered the phone. Ebony began to explain what had happened. "Well someone stole his." "Is that all you can say. I see the fruit don't fall far from the tree. You stole his money, so it's ok to take someone else's shit?" "I don't like talking to you. You make me angry," he said. This wasn't about neither one of them; this was about parenting. This nigga done fell and bumped his head.

Since Ebony could see that Shawn wasn't been taught any damn thing, she couldn't hold that against him. Malcolm and her decided to let him enjoy himself and take him to the park. The two of them acted like kids riding every rollercoaster they had there, while Ebony found some shade. Ebony knew she had to come up with some kind of way to get Shawn out of the grips of this monster.

Chapter 16

Once Shawn left, Ebony still had the glow. However; things began to change a little. Malcolm was starting to act strange. Ebony kept forging ahead hoping that Malcolm would overcome his fear and just relinquish all his love to her. Something was holding him back, and he would stop himself when trying to get it across to her. "Never mind"! This left her at a lost.

As much as she loved this man, something had to give. She tried to put herself in his shoes. Patience! She had learned plenty of patience dealing with her own tragedies. Deep in her heart, Ebony knew that Malcolm was placed there for a reason. After the encounter with Maze, Ebony felt as though she was ready for real love.

On bended knees, she asked that the next man that entered her world was to be her soul mate. Why would he block something that was predestined to be? At no time did she ever lose her faith. Thru tragic times, she pulled strength from the **"most high."**

Love is a compromise. Whatever made Malcolm think that Ebony was a child was far from reality. Ebony had traveled around the world at a young age. Picking up different pieces of diverse cultures life had to offer. She was trained in discipline thru her military experience. Eventually, she had graduated with her BS in Business. Ebony was ahead of her time and could hold a conversation with any person. For some reason, he always played the role that he knew everything. Being older gives you some wisdom, but not to all of life's situations.

Emotions can often time over rule logic when it comes to matters of the heart. You lose focus and lose your way. She tried to get her point across. Learning the hard way, she learned never to let anyone walk all over her again, thanks to Lawrence. This girl would argue her point. Someday a lawyer would probably emerge out of all this. Ebony was tired of people stepping on the little people. Someone had to fight for them. She had become an advocate for younger women going through the same things she had. Often times, she never shared her story, but something inside of her wanted to release all of the anger, hatred and frustration that was bottled up inside of her.

Chapter 17

Staying in close quarters together for the third time, Ebony began to see the real Malcolm. He began to disappear for hours at a time in Mexico. She didn't give it a second thought. Not until the luau. Ebony had to admit when she had a couple of drinks, she was a happy soul. Granted if you said something out the way, she would tell it to you straight. After dining and drinking, upon walking to the room Malcolm said something smart. The liquor had taken into effect and she blurted out how she really felt. This only fueled the fire and he left her by herself. The change began that night. He asked for it! Malcolm believed that he could talk shit and for people to let it slide all the time. That night once she finally made it back, he was on the balcony. Really she could have cared less. Wasn't like he was knocking her down with the sex anyway. It was best he did sleep his ass on the patio.

The end was drawing near. Ebony could sense it. As hard as she gave all her love, Malcolm kept rejecting it. It made her question her sensuality. All sorts of things ran thru her mind. "I ain't Halle Berry, but I damn sure ain't butt fuck ugly either." "If he doesn't want me, why waste time?" In her eyesight, life was too short. She needed someone that had a sensitive side at times, not just when the mood suited them. Any and every time Ebony wanted to do something or be intimate, the answer was a flat out "NO". Ebony couldn't understand why. She didn't know what could be wrong. Did she lose the beauty that once attracted him to her? She was his Beyoncé or had he forgotten! Malcolm meant the world to her, always had.

The conclusion was she had to let him go. Ebony didn't want to lose herself and all she worked so hard to get back. The stronger she professed her love to him, the more he pushed away. This was a hurting feeling in the worst kind of way.

Ebony had become a fighter. At this point in the game, she had surrendered to love. Years of searching for true love and now this. Giving the fact that she had dealt with an abusive marriage, father not being in her life, mother and stepfather passing away and to top it off, still having to deal with Lawrence's bullshit of not being able to talk to Shawn; the pain of letting the first person she ever fell in love with go, would be tragic. Fantasia said it best "this shit is Bittersweet."

As Ebony overlooked the ocean and the waves made the calming sound, it soothed her soul. "This too shall pass," Ebony thought. Tears streamed down her face as she looked at the blue-ish green water. "You can't keep someone that doesn't want to be kept!" In her mind, once they touched down in Baltimore, they would depart for good. The memories of the love she shared with Malcolm would be just that. MEMORIES! They would forever be etched in her heart.

Two things she would take out of this relationship: 1. It was better to have loved than never have loved at all. 2. Ebony was capable of letting her guard down and really give her heart to someone. Ebony would leave the pain in the blue waters and emerge home as a new woman. Ready to conquer whatever this world had to offer.

Trying to get over the pain of losing her one true love, Ebony just felt a lil down and out. She called Christal from Mexico and confided what had transpired on her journey. Christal told her that her man did the same thing to her, and Ebony shouldn't pay his ass no damn mind. He would eventually come around. With every beat of Ebony's heart she really was in love with this man and wanted it to work. But, with his attitude that he couldn't be struck by love, it became unbearable. For a minute, she thought she was relieving the episode with Lawrence. The only difference was that she was never in love with her ex-husband.

The last day of the vacation, he left out the room without saying a word. She was glad to be going home. Ebony thought that while there, it should have been passionate love making, laughter, joy and sightseeing. It was anything but. Nothing! She could have gone by her damn self; if she knew that his mood would change. She basically felt like she was alone anyway. Malcolm had spoiled the last three days of the vacation for no apparent reason. His attitude was like flickering a light switch on and off.

He entered the room to ask if they were going to breakfast. Ebony didn't have a problem with it, considering they didn't even eat together the night before. At the dining facility, he just sat there and didn't say a word. Neither did he eat. What was the purpose of going then?

Once returning back to the room to gather their belongings for checkout, "You can't hear motherfucker." "Excuse me, what did you say?" "You heard me motherfucker!" Ebony couldn't believe her ears. Then again, she didn't know what was wrong with this man. He must have fell and bumped his fucking head. "That's the last time you will curse at me for no reason." She just grabbed her bags and left the room. Glad to be going home, she checked out at the registration desk and headed towards the waiting area for the van. Ebony placed her headphones on and tried to drown her pain in the music. Malcolm approached her, but she had no words for him at that point. He must have thought he was talking to a child. Malcolm practically had the nerve to lean in for a kiss. Hell to the NO! Ebony had about had it with his ass at this point. He had spoiled her birthday week with bullshit drama that wasn't even necessary. Whatever fucking problems he had, he could have left that shit in Baltimore. The whole ride to the airport, he wanted to chat. Ebony had nothing to say. She just wanted the love to be washed away in the ocean.

Touchdown! Baltimore here she was, ready to let this forsaken nightmare end. As they went to the baggage claim, their luggage was on a different flight. Christal had come to pick them up, and Ebony just said fuck the luggage. She could get her's the following day. Ebony didn't put two and two together. Malcolm was adamant about waiting. He gave her and Christal money to go to G & M's for crab cakes. That was the least he could do for all the shit he did wrong in Cancun. The two ladies drove off and Ebony began to tell her aunt what went down.

It dawned on her the reason he wanted his luggage so bad, was the alcohol that he had purchased. The whole thing clicked, this motherfucker was an alcoholic. His whole demeanor changed after he had drinks. Ebony couldn't see it at first because he kept it hidden so well. It was too late; she had fallen in love already. How was she going to shake this nigga? She knew she had too; she couldn't live like that again.

Two days after returning home, back to the jewelry store she went. If his unappreciative ass didn't know how to act, then why waste her money. Showing her deep compassionate love for him, she had even purchased him a ring. Ebony wanted to be committed to this man. Good thing this trip woke her dumb ass up. Since it was her birthday, Ebony exchanged it for something she would treasure for eternity. A charm bracelet for her growth as the woman she would eventually become. Something was better for her out there. Once again she needed to take the damn blinders off and wake up. The question was, "could she?"

Ebony wanted to hurt in peace and move on with her life. Deep inside she had always loved this man, but him taking her through the hot and cold changes she was not willing to accept. The two had been in Baltimore now for about five days. No call or anything, which was good for her. The day that she decided to meet Christal for drinks, the phone rings. Malcolm asked could he stop by to get his belongings that were left at her home. Ebony didn't have a problem with that. She had promised to meet Christal at 10:30. Exiting the shower, the doorbell rang. Ebony knew that it was Malcolm. *This shit shouldn't take long! He could get his shit and go."*

As she approached the door to give him his belongings, he smelt like pure liquor. All you had to do was light a match to his ass and he probably would have blown up. Ebony already had his stuff bagged up. Never in a million years would she expect what was going to happen to her. Déjà vu! For some reason Malcolm wasn't ready to end this on a good note. Just wanting to get dressed and leave out her house, the unimaginable happened.

Malcolm pushed Ebony hard that she fell back into the loveseat. She didn't even see it coming. Lawrence had taught her well! Ebony wasn't going to let it go down like that. She regained her composure and hit the fuck out of him with all her might. All she wanted now was him to get the fuck out of her house. He had lost his ever loving mind.

Was it a setup to learn all that you can about a person's life to use it against them? Ebony wasn't ready to go back to jail and lose everything that she worked hard for, but he kept pushing the issue. "I ain't going a motherfucking place. Call the fuckin police Washington. I still ain't leaving." Liquor turns some people into monsters and trust and believe, one was staring her in the eye.

At that point, Ebony went upstairs to the bathroom to light up a cigarette. As Malcolm followed her, she had phoned his mother. Ebony never had a chance to say anything before Malcolm grabbed the phone out her hand and threw it to floor. She could see that the call connected, "Just leave my house would you. Get your stuff and go," Ebony said. "Fuck that, you are going to listen to me!"

All bets were off at that moment. As she left and went into her spare bedroom to get away, he followed her. Ebony sat down on the bed and before you know it, Malcolm had a strange look in his eye. "You like hitting me." Malcolm had slapped the shit out of Ebony. It was do or die now!! The survival mode had kicked in. Ebony landed a few punches and continued to swing on him with all her might. As he fell to the floor, she had him cornered between the bed and the dresser. At that moment she wrapped her legs around his neck. Her adrenaline was pumping as Ebony tried to squeeze the life out of his ass. He better been glad she wasn't in her bedroom because she would have stabbed Malcolm at that moment. Malcolm began to beg, "I am sorry baby, just let me up. I am leaving." Get the fuck out!

While approaching downstairs for him to leave, the house phone rang. It was Malcolm's mother asking, was he still there in the house? She had heard the whole episode. As Ebony proceeded to give him the phone, he hung it up. She called back again, and once again he hung up on his own mother.

Before he exited the house, Malcolm took Ebony's cell phone. He knew she didn't have anyone's phone number without it. Malcolm's mother called again. Ebony didn't want to bother her, but she just wanted her cell phone back. His mother called him, but he claimed that he left it in Ebony's doorway. Ebony went outside and nothing. This had put a damper in her mood of going out! Damn! *I can't believe this shit. Am I still with Lawrence or what? This motherfucker got it twisted. I have left him alone and now this. Naw, that ain't called for.* Ebony was talking out loud to herself. Twenty minutes later, the doorbell rang again. Ebony wasn't stupid; she wasn't letting him in her home. He finally got the message and left the phone in the doorway.

After that fiasco, Ebony didn't know what to make of Malcolm anymore. This was the man that she broke down her wall and gave her devoting love too. Ashanti had said it best "my days are long without you, but I am hurting while I'm with you; and though my heart can't take no more, I keep on running back to you." This is how Ebony felt. She still was dealing with Lawrence's mental abuse. It seemed like the cycle was now with her and Malcolm. She thought, "When will the drama end?" Getting rid of one abuser and finding another. *Did she wear a sign on her head, Abuse me please?* What had she done in this life that was so bad, that she had to keep enduring all this pain? Ebony just screamed, Calgon take me away!

Trying to make a fresh new start was going to be difficult; but Ebony had overcome this kind of situation before. It was going to take time. It had taken her ten years to actually wake up and get the hell out of dodge with Lawrence. She didn't know how long for Malcolm to get out of her system. The only problem, Ebony hadn't reached rock bottom yet!!

Chapter 18

How do you mend a broken heart? No one truly knows, but in Ebony's book, everything had to go! First she sat in the barber chair and let it all fall to the floor. She didn't know if that was a symbolic thing, but Malcolm had worried her so much like Lawrence did, her hair was once again falling out. The tremendous amount of stress was once again on her shoulders. Boy did Ebony need strength! The only one that could provide it was **"GOD."** This game of love that she been in search for all her life was breaking her down. Malcolm still would not leave this woman alone. If he couldn't handle the commitment of being in love, than just let it be! It had been two weeks after the physical abuse, he had called again. Love was blinded for the second time around. She hadn't gotten over him and really wanted him in her life, but changes definitely had to be made. As she listened to him apologize, he stated that he was going to get his act together. Ebony didn't ask for much, but damn! The two chatted for an hour and Ebony suggested that he go to Alcoholic Anonymous meetings. He reluctantly agreed. While at work, she began research and printed off some places that he should call for treatment.

In the midst of their conversation out of the blue, his mood changed just that quick! Malcolm told her "don't ask me who I am sleeping with because I don't ask you." This cut her like a knife. As a couple or so she thought in her mind, they shouldn't be sleeping with anyone else period. Technically, was he Ebony's man after all that had transpired? It wasn't like he was touching her in that department.

Not even thinking about the consequences or repercussions of her actions, she picked up the phone. Boy toy! Here we go again! It had been a while since she had seen or spoken to Maze. Ebony needed intervention to help her not to turn to this young man. The sad part was she had half of a man and was still lonely.

Before you knew it, the text had gone thru. "Can I see you?" "When?" "Today or tomorrow, your choice" "Tonight!" It was on and popping. Ebony dotted off and jumped in her ride heading towards home. Just the thought of getting it in mattered. Not that bullshit of a one minute encounter. She really needed someone that was going to put it down on her.

Maze showed up right on time, 12:15. Once she glanced at his dimples, the girl knew her stress level was about to subside. Malcolm with his words and non-chalant attitude pushed her to this freakin point. Maze knew what time it was! That's what they always did. If she wanted to release stress and fuck, he was game. This young thoroughbred gave it all he had. Ebony was time enough for his ass though. She always made sure she left his ass out of breath and not wanting to go another round. By the third round, Maze couldn't take it anymore. "I am done for the night," he said. As Ebony laid in his arms, it felt so good. Even though she was dealing with Malcolm's bullshit, at least the last three hours took her mind off it.

Once Maze left, Ebony blew out the candles and snuggled up to the pillow. Deep inside, this didn't solve anything for her. Her problems would still be there, but this made the night's sleep worthwhile.

With a well-rested and peaceful sleep under her belt; everything was going good til the phone rang. Malcolm as usual wanting to argue;

he was fucking up her high. Damn! Did Malcolm and Lawrence go to the same school? After chatting with him, he didn't want to hear anything that she was saying. That control shit again!

Ebony was tired of the bull and began to lay it on thick. "If you can fuck, so can I! I had no problem getting it in last night." You could feel the uneasiness in his voice, but he tried to play it off. She knew she hurt him, but Ebony wanted him to hurt just as bad. There has got to be a better way than to play games with grown ass people. Everyone was an adult. If it doesn't work, get another. Love can only sustain you for so long, and then you have to just hurt and move on.

Ebony thought that if he could say fucking hurtful things to her, now it was time to turn the tables on him. She was tired of playing everyone else's game. If she was going to do something it was going to benefit her and make her happy.

A week later after leaving Christal's house one night; Ebony pulled onto her block. She always watched her surroundings. Ebony saw a car ride down the street slowly and turn. Ebony thought it was Malcolm's car, but couldn't really see it. She didn't think anything of it, until the lights from a car approached her. This wasn't unusual; she did live on a public street.

The car slowly approached her car, and Ebony was preparing herself for whatever. If she had to cut something up, she had no problem. If anything was coming for her, she damn well was going to put up a fight. The car blocked Ebony in so she couldn't get out. "Malcolm what do you want?"

As he pulled down the street and doubled parked the car, Ebony didn't know what to think! She knew that she wasn't letting him inside of the house. Malcolm had given back the key before the fight, and after what transpired, oh no! He could say whatever outside.

Malcolm began to cry as he apologized for his behavior. Ebony stood there and listened to his excuses. "I have been driving around looking for you. I wanted to leave a note on your door, but you pulled up. I am really sorry. Don't know what came over me. Haven't been able to sleep just kept thinking about the situation getting out of hand."

The rain began to come down; Ebony accepted the apology and gave Malcolm a hug. "I can't be your friend because I am still in love with you, but I wish you nothing but the best. You need to get help for your drinking; it's not solving your problems." As Ebony made her way to her front door, she just shook her head. She hadn't even got upstairs before her phone rang "I love you. This is killing me!" That night all Ebony could do was pray for him.

Since last week of being with Maze, Ebony's mind was mentally wrapped around tonight. Maze was coming through, and the long anticipated encounter was going to go down that night. "Malcolm, who? Malcolm, what?" She kept thinking, midnight and the shit is going to be on and popping. Maze was supposed to call her two hours before to make sure she was up.

Just the thought of the sparring session had her up beforehand. As Ebony entered into the bathroom to begin pampering herself for the nights events; the phone rang. Fuck! What the hell do he (Malcolm) want now? Could he sense something was up? Ebony answered the phone, trying to play it off like she was sleep. That didn't faze his ass. "I am on my way!" "Damn it! This motherfucker is crazy. I can't let Maze get caught up in that. Malcolm is known for carrying his gun. Especially after the incident that we had, Maze don't need to be in the mix of this."

"Don't come! Please don't come! Call me when you get this text. Mommie will make it up to Daddy later." Ebony was frantic about the situation. She didn't know what Malcolm was capable of at this point.

The doorbell rang ten minutes later, and in walks Malcolm. Ebony played it off, but was pissed as hell. The two chatted and Malcolm began to take off his clothes and lay down in the bed. She was shocked! For some reason, Malcolm kept getting out the bed. Ebony never paid any attention to it. Finally as Malcolm began to make love to her; Malcolm stopped within a minute. "Damn! He knew how to fuck up a good thing. Been waiting for what seemed like forever, now this. Oh, hell no!"

Just that quick this asshole, put his clothes on and left. Ebony couldn't believe what had just transpired. She was in total shock. Once he abruptly left, he then had the nerve to call with some bullshit. "It just didn't feel right. Something felt like it jumped off you onto me!" "What the fuck did he mean by that? I don't even sleep around and on top of that, I always get checked. He the one that couldn't get his dick hard; now he wanna pawn that shit off on me. Hell naw!"

Pissed wasn't the word for how Ebony felt. She had missed out on a three hour sparring session for a one minute fiasco. All she could think of the New Year was around the corner, and she would have to put this thing to rest once and for all.

Chapter 19

Malcolm began calling her everyday like he had before, like nothing was wrong. Being gullible as usual, Ebony fell into the devilish trap once again. He was being so nice and sincere. Thanksgiving was approaching and he wanted her to go to his family's dinner. She had met the family before at his cookouts, but never this personable. Thinking he was trying to change, she accepted the invitation.

Thanksgiving day, after spending time with her own family; she set out to meet Malcolm. Arriving at his sister's house, the butterflies began to hit the pit of her stomach. Granted his mother knew what had spiraled out of control, but did the rest of the family? His family welcomed her with open arms. Twenty minutes of begin there, his mother arrived. "How are you Ebony?" Ebony explained that Malcolm had done a dramatic change. "Don't get use to it, he'll slip up again." "Well I am going to ride the niceness train til it stop."

Three days later, the two of them were off to Georgetown in D.C. Malcolm wanted to locate this jazz club for future reference. Ebony was down for going, to get out the house. As the two arrived, Ebony was shocked that Malcolm grabbed and held her hand. The gentleman in him was emerging. Where had all this been hiding? It had been going downhill since they had first started this venture of love together. These were the things he should have been doing all along. The two settled down for an outstanding lunch at a quaint little restaurant. It had been a while since his last outburst or sudden changes.

Making the trip back to B-more, the two stopped off to Whitemarsh Mall. Ebony had some last minute Christmas presents to get for Shawn. Malcolm was pumped also. He asked what else her son needed. The two went into Old Navy and Malcolm purchased a pea coat for Shawn. Knowing that her money was limited, but wanted to make sure her son had a memorable holiday; Ebony was grateful. It was like Malcolm was on a spending spree. The two hit Dr. Vision Works. Ebony was glad Malcolm wanted to update his look. She didn't fall in love with the glasses, but the man. The glasses he wore made him look old. Beyoncé, "Upgrade you." It didn't take her long to pick out two pairs. The glasses made him look about ten years younger. Begin a harsh man, Malcolm didn't want to spend that kind of money on himself. The two left the store, but Ebony was headed back to at least get one pair as a gift.

Malcolm finally came to the conclusion that his woman had been right. He politely gave her the Discover. As she approached the salesperson, she caught the tail end of his conversation with his co-worker "He wasn't willing to pay for them." "Excuse me, but don't ever underestimate the power of a woman. Now can I get the two pair of glasses?"

The two had a couple more stops to make. Driving to Wal-Mart, Malcolm wanted to buy Shawn that IPod. Remembering what Shawn had done over the summer, he wanted him to have his own. Ebony couldn't see spending that kind of money for possibly Lawrence to take it from Shawn. She talked him into a MP3 instead. Ebony felt more comfortable with that to say the least.

Last stop, then home. It had been a long day and she was getting tired. Ebony made her way to McDonalds for a smoothie and Malcolm to the lottery store. Once arriving at her door, "Now get the fuck out." At that moment, Ebony should have listened to his mother. She was the realist person besides her own mother that she knew. He had just messed up a perfectly good day. If this shit was meant to be a joke, she didn't find it fucking funny. Ebony grabbed her shit out the car and never looked back. No she didn't feel bad for the money he had just spent, this made up for his nasty ass mouth.

Out of the blue Malcolm's mood changed and he began to lash out at Ebony. "Never call my fucking house again!" She didn't have time for that rampage shit again, she disconnected the line. Ebony thought to herself "not a problem." "I am not going to let anyone spoil my time with my son." You want to have faith and believe in a person, but when they show you no change you gotta let it go. In the words of Tina Turner "What's Love Got to do With It."

The plan was for all three (Malcolm, Ebony and Shawn) to spend the holiday together. During the talks with her son, Ebony explained that she had a friend. Shawn blurted "Mr. Malcolm." Damn children can be real cleaver. At this point in the game, Ebony was not willing to let her son see this dysfunctional relationship Malcolm and her shared. Shawn had been through too much as it was.

The following morning before she could get out the bed good, the phone began to ring. "Open the front door." Ebony was too damn tired to argue. "What the fuck did he want now?" She made her way to the door and in walks Malcolm with a big bag. Inside was two sweatsuits for her son. He wanted to see all that she had purchased for her child. In the back of her mind, she wondered what the hell for? This was her child not his. Not wanting a scene, she pulled out Shawn's stuff. "When Shawn arrives, I will get him some boots and sneakers."

It was whatever in her mind; at that point she could care less. Going back to bed was her main priority. Malcolm always claimed the two was going to do this or that and the day would come to do it, "That ain't gonna happen," he would say. This was another one of his full of himself moments.

Chapter 20

The middle of December rolled around, and Ebony hadn't heard from Malcolm since the shopping spree and that was fine with her. At this point, the only thing that mattered was getting Shawn. It had been at least ten Christmas holidays missed. Lawrence made sure of that. No one and nothing was going to stand in the way, not even Malcolm. She knew he would eventually call to get under her skin. Sure enough the week before Shawn was to arrive; the phone rang while she was at work. "What time are you leaving and do you still want me to go?" Ebony could give a flying fuck at this point. No man would come between her and her child. She would go to the ends of the earth for her son. She always had and this time was no different.

Never in a million years did Ebony think that her and Malcolm would turn out like this. She knew he had her best interest at heart when they were friends, but now every other week he was cursing her out for some reason. Ebony just cried to herself. "How could someone that always helps people get treated this way?"

Shawn's coming for Christmas!!!! This would be the most joyous moment at this point in her life. The only reason he was sending Shawn for Christmas, because Ebony was determined to take his black ass back to court. He needed something to show to the judge. This bitch was off her rocker anyway. Even Ray Charles could see that this fucker was a liar! Deep down in her heart she knew that if she had money to afford a lawyer, she would eat his ass alive. But his muthafuckin day was approaching.

Time was running out on Lawrence's ass. What was he gonna do when Shawn turned 18 and left his stupid ass? The child support would be gone and the most feared thing in his life would come true. Shawn would move to be with his mother.

Sometimes people need to be careful what they do to other people. Karma is a mother, what goes around comes around! If only Ebony could keep still and know that the end was coming near. Deep down she knew that it was, but her baby needed her. Any woman would fight until they couldn't fight anymore when it came to their children. That's what Ebony intended to do! Not a day would go by without her thinking of some way to get Shawn with her.

Children's lives are critical at the younger years and they pick up habits from their environment. Shawn was not learning anything, but to lie, steal and gamble his way through life, just like his father. This is a cold cruel world and without an education, he will be lost. Even now, most people with an education are finding it hard to find a job.

Shawn sort of has his head on straight. He wants to go to college and become a professional football player. Ebony tries to encourage him every time she would see or talk to him. Education is key!

Countdown! She talked to Shawn and to her surprise; he claimed that he had tried on two occasions to call her. Ebony never received a call at all. Shawn finally told her that his dad told him he had to dial a one first. Ebony thought to herself, "What the fuck is Lawrence teaching him. At fifteen, you can't even dial the phone correctly." This was even more of an incentive to keep instilling things in him every chance she could. Shawn was so excited and he wanted Christmas to be here soon. If only! They both felt like they needed to be with one another!

Ebony was anticipating the arrival of her son. Granted she had to make that long drive to pick him up, it would be well worth it. And since she no longer was taking Malcolm with her, it would give her time to reflect on the issues at hand. All she could think about was the cooking and putting up the Christmas tree. Waiting for the look on her child's face on Christmas morning. Times were tight, but she managed to charge some shit up. She would just have to pay the piper when the time came. She wanted to make sure that this was the best Christmas Shawn would have since he had become the age of remembrance.

Two days before picking up Shawn, Lawrence sent Ebony an email stating that he had problems with his vehicle. If it ain't one thing it's another. After the fiasco last summer with Lawrence's transportation and now this. Ebony didn't care how the fuck he was going to get to Kings Dominion with her child, but he better do what he had to! This was just a ploy for her to lash out and for him to take the paper to court. Since the court date was fast approaching in February, Lawrence was only letting Shawn come up for that particular reason. He needed some kind of leg to stand on. The judge believed his ass all the time anyway. The court kept telling Ebony to keep records; when she provided them, shit gets dismissed anyway. What was the use?

Pumped up and ready, Ebony was preparing to take this ride. Coordination with Lawrence was always a hindrance. She asked if she could get her son early due to the holiday traffic. Since his trip was shorter than hers, she would call hitting the D.C. area. Ebony had talked to Shawn and told him just to bring himself. Lawrence needed to confirm this with his ex-wife. No doubt, it ain't like he sent him with a haircut or clean clothes, anyway! In her mind, Lawrence was getting like these trifling ass women. Get the child support money, and spend it on themselves or their current man or woman.

Today was the day of joy. Bringing her baby home for the holidays was all she really cared about. Tired and drained, Ebony didn't care. Running on pure adrenaline, she was out the door at 8 a.m. Around 8:30 she placed a call to her ex. Even getting stuck in traffic for an hour, she still beat them there. *My three hour trip to his hour and a half and his ass is getting child support. What the fuck! I think this arrangement is useless; he is always late. Shawn is old enough to fly and get here in forty minutes. I spend more damn time on the road than with my child.* Lawrence was still holding all the cards. *Today out of all days, I ain't going to let nothing spoil this for me,* she said to herself. *It's all worth the wait! Even if I have to drive all the way to Virginia Beach today, I don't care at this moment.* Negative thoughts really began to cloud her mind as she waited for what seemed like an eternity. *It ain't like he can treat my son like I can. He wants to be better at motherhood than me, but he can't. Pussy will always rule his world.* At that moment the two pulled up, every thought she had, flew straight out the window.

Ebony didn't stick around for the wanna be cordial shit. Once Shawn put his foot in the car, his mother had the car in drive. He had grown more than the last time she'd seen him. Riding up the road, Ebony laid out activities for the day. First was to put up a tree. Ebony never put up a tree since she had left them. She made sure the day her baby came home, she would have one. Shawn had also told his mother, "don't do anything without me."

This girl was nothing but smiles. She had her big baby home and he was like a kid in a candy store once again. Ebony watched as Shawn decorated the tree. Even though she was tired, she still had to start preparing dinner for the following day.

It was one more place that she wanted to take him, Miracle on 34th St. The family including the dog hopped in the car, and off they went. Shawn was in awe. He even had a big ass grin on his face. Shawn was just glad to be home. Ebony had told her son that she was broke, but the only present that they had was under the tree. Ebony had left out some small stuff that she had wrapped up. "Mommie, I don't care. As long as I am here with you this Christmas, gifts don't mean anything. I got my Christmas gift and that is you." Ebony wanted to break down and cry.

Chapter 21

The girl arose bright and early Christmas Eve. The pots and pans were slinging on the stove. Ebony didn't know when the last time she threw down like this in the kitchen. It had been a long time, but now there was good reason.

Given the fact that Malcolm was a jerk, Ebony tried hard to compromise. She reached out to him because Shawn kept asking for him. Shawn and Malcolm had created a tight knit bond over the course of the years. Going against her better judgment, she called. It was Christmas Eve and the two had planned to show Shawn what a happy family consisted off. The plan was for all three to sit down and have a good dinner.

Malcolm. being the jackass he was, only spoke to Shawn. He wished Shawn a "Merry Christmas" and told him that he would speak to him before he left to go back home. Ebony tried!

The two sat down at the table and grubbed like they had never eaten before.

"Mommie, this food is delicious," Shawn said. "Baby, ya'll don't have meals like this for the holidays?" Ebony inquired. "Dad cooks," he replied, "but it is nothing like this." Since the two had stuffed their faces with good ole' ham, greens, string beans, mash potatoes, baked macaroni, baked chicken, stuffing and yams, they barely had room for the sweet potato pies Ebony had made. Shawn went upstairs and took a nap. Ebony was tired also. She knew she had to get up in the morning to make a dish to take to work.

As the night fell and both retired for bed for the night; Ebony had to make sure Shawn was truly asleep. She peeked into his bedroom and he was a goner. She snuck down the stairs about three. She went into the closet as quietly as she could and got straight to work. Ebony had bought her baby clothes out the ying-yang. She wanted to see the surprise on her son's face that morning. Ebony laid all the outfits over the sofa and moved his gifts from under the tree, on top of the clothes. After she was satisfied by the display, she snuck back upstairs.

The following morning as she got up to put some macaroni in the oven for work, Ebony heard Shawn in the bathroom. *This boy don't wake up early for nothing. Is it because it's Christmas that he has gotten out of his bed at seven?* Shawn had made it down the stairs.

"Good morning, Merry Christmas baby." Ebony ran in the kitchen to make sure the noodles weren't burning and before Ebony could get the camera good, to see the reaction on his face; he had already started trying his stuff on. The initial shock overwhelmed him. "You used to get stuff like this when I lived with you. Your Christmas' are not like this now?" "Mom, I have never seen so much stuff in my life!" Ebony was happy because her baby was happy.

"Call your Dad!" she said. Ebony didn't want to be selfish like Lawrence had been over the years. "I did, Mom, he asked what did I get. I told him a lot of clothes and everything. He said he bought me a new phone." *My $400 a month and all he could get him was a damn phone. I bet his girlfriend got more than that, selfish bastard.*

Before Ebony left to go to work, Shawn went with Barbara to eat dinner at her cousin's in Pennsylvania. Shawn would get to see all his family there and spend quality time with them. Ebony missed out, but she had to work. As long as her child was happy, it really didn't matter.

Ring, Ring! What the hell does he (Malcolm) want? "Where is my son?" This motherfucker was drunk. Now all of a sudden he wanna know where Shawn was. Didn't she give him plenty of time to get it together for her child's sake? "Don't fuckin' call on Christmas and want to play daddy now." Ebony disconnected the line.

The phone rang again! Malcolm just wanted to argue, as usual. *This was a joyous holiday and he had fucked it up, don't be badgering me with bullshit.* Ebony was plain out tired. She could feel her pressure rising. Malcolm's last girlfriend had passed away while talking to him on the phone; Ebony didn't want to be his next victim. "You probably killed her with the words you spit out your mouth, but I be damned if I let you kill me." Ebony disconnected the line once again! Didn't she try to compromise with his ass?

Two days later, Malcolm called and asked to speak to Shawn. The next thing she knew, Shawn was hitting the shower. Ebony wanted to know what was going on. "Mr. Malcolm is picking me up." Once again, she didn't know how this man could treat her like shit, but catered to her child. As Shawn left, Ebony gave him Malcolm's presents.

Once at work, Shawn called to tell his mother that he had gone to Pennsylvania once again and Malcolm had purchased him some tennis shoes. In Ebony's book, that was for all the foul shit he done to her. She just wanted to be happy for her child. Malcolm called her and talked like he had some sense. "I would like to go with you to the party tomorrow." "Whatever," Ebony thought but she didn't say no.

Chapter 22

Malcolm picked Ebony up at 6 o'clock sharp. The two were venturing out once again as a couple to Ebony's aunt's birthday party. Shawn stayed home, but he and Malcolm somehow devised a plan to watch the football game that night.

The club was jumping and the place was packed. It was happy hour! To Ebony's surprise, Malcolm was very attentive to her that night. "I wanna treat you like the queen, you are," Malcolm stated. Laying another damn trap for Ebony, but she couldn't see into his bullshit. She fell for it again. Damn it! Ebony sucked every ounce of it up; forgetting how he acted like a jackass two days before.

As the drinks were flowing, somehow Malcolm came out of his shell. He began to dance. Ebony laughed her ass off, cause he had no fuckin' rhythm. It was just a different side that she had never seen before. A smiling Malcolm whispered in her ear, "I love you. Thank you for being there for me."

In the heat of the moment all the shit he had done to her, flew out the window. She dropped her guard down again. Her defenses were weakened by his niceness. Having a wonderful time Ebony didn't think that the night could go wrong. She was gonna keep her fingers crossed.

The two had been at the club about an hour when Malcolm told her; he made a promise to Shawn that he would be back by 9 p.m. Cut the fun she was having out, but anything for her son. The two said their goodbyes to the family that had gathered for the occasion.

After they arrived back to the house, Ebony went upstairs and laid in the bed. Malcolm made his way in the basement with Shawn. It's funny how he kept his promises to her son, but never to her. Malcolm was the only man that Shawn had really seen around his mother for a long period of time. Ebony was adamant about not having different men around her child.

Apparently Ebony must have drifted off to sleep. She awoke to Malcolm entering the room with his pj's on. Oh snap! Now he really wanna be the loving family man to this woman. The door closed and locked behind him. Ebony just turned over and went back to sleep. Malcolm laid down next to her and began to kiss her gently. She didn't know what lit a match under his ass, but he wanted to make love. Ebony rolled with it. Shit, Maze had her ass on punishment since last month; and Malcolm seldom got in the mood to touch her.

The softness that she fell in love with was back. He caressed her body like when they were sneaking around. *Shawn needed to be here on a permanent basis, if he's gonna be nice like this,* Ebony thought. Malcolm's soft hands explored her body as he slid off her nightgown. Part of her thought that it was gonna be over before it began. He fooled her ass! He was the person that she fell in love with over the summer. The man that used his hands with the softest touch to entice her mind before he even had taken his clothes off. That's the man that she wanted back. The one that had her cumming just from the intimacy and not penetration. That's the wondrous thing that had her: hook, line and sinker back then. Sure enough, Malcolm pulled out the stops again.

Ebony didn't want to spoil the mood, but where had this passion been hiding? Flashbacks of the summer flooded her mind. The thoughts of the two sneaking around when Shawn wasn't home. It was more of the intimate moments and the passionate kisses that captured her heart. The game of keeping it a secret from her son was the ultimate high. Those precious moments etched in her heart and mind.

Malcolm gently kissed Ebony and looked into her brown eyes. All she could see was that he truly loved her, but the mood swings won the battle everytime. The two made passionate love that night.

That voodoo shit he put on her ass last night, made her rise early as hell the next morning. The girl was in the kitchen cooking both of her men breakfast. The three sat down as a family. Ebony just monitored Shawn's reactions. She basically didn't do any talking. On the inside Ebony felt blessed to have this family unit, she always dreamt of.

Once Malcolm left, Ebony asked Shawn "How did you feel seeing Mr. Malcolm spend the night with me?" Her son simply answered, "I didn't have a problem with it." She just wanted to make sure that she took her child's feelings into consideration. This little week had gone by so fast; tomorrow, it was time for her child to go home.

Loading the car up that morning, Ebony was once again sad to see her child leaving. Overall, she did enjoy having him there with her regardless of the bad start with Malcolm. As Malcolm pulled up to the door, Shawn got excited! The three took their sweet little time getting to K.D. Shit his father was always late, so they figured why not make him wait.

Ebony and Shawn went into Cracker Barrel and ate; while Malcolm caught a nap in the car. Lawrence kept calling Shawn's phone, like he was in a rush. "Daddy we are stuck in traffic." Ebony knew her son was lying but didn't care at that moment. *Make that ass wait. For all the low down dirty shit, fuck that trick he rushing back too. I am going to soak up every minute that I can with my child,* Ebony thought.

The three arrived in about twenty minutes. Usually Lawrence gets out the truck to help Shawn get his things, but when Malcolm is around he sits and stares. Ebony ran into the restroom before getting back on the road. Malcolm had gone to play the lottery. Once Ebony came out the store, Shawn had all his stuff in the truck. Ebony gave her son a big hug and kiss. "I love you baby. Call me when you get home." Being a big baby herself, she wanted to cry.

Shawn stood there as Ebony got into the passenger seat. She was wondering what he was waiting for. He didn't move until Malcolm came out the store. Shawn gave Malcolm a big hug also. If only you could see the fire coming out of Lawrence? He was madder than the devil in the hot pits of hell. Pulling off was really hard for Ebony, she just faced the window with sadness. Her heart had been torn apart once again.

Malcolm had planned on bringing in the New Year with Ebony. They didn't like hanging out much, so they decided on church. Maybe bringing in a New Year together, would aspire change. Things were going good, so Ebony thought. She had gotten a little sick with a cold, but thought that Malcolm would take care of her. He had called a couple of times during New Year's Day to check on her, but never showed. During one of the calls, you could tell he was drunk. Once again he started talking crazy shit. Ebony just hung up the phone. How can you enjoy a good day at church, and then become an asshole?

The following morning about six o'clock the phone rang. "Come to the door." Ebony didn't want to get out of bed because she was feeling bad. Malcolm kept persisting that she open up the door because he had left something. "I will get it when I wake up," she said. "No come now," he insisted.

As Ebony dragged her body down the stairs to open the door, it was a bag hanging outside of the locked storm door. "This motherfucker left my personal shit from his house outside. At least I gave him the opportunity to come to my house and get his shit. Oh a fucking note!" It read, "I can't do this. This is a New Year and I just can't do this. Here is lunch money." *A measly ass $10. Fuck that! I am more upset that I let my fucking guard down again and to be in church talking about how I suppose to be his queen and two days later now this shit.*

Hot and pissed off! Ebony got herself together and just drove to church. That was the only place she was going to find solace. There had to be a word there for her. The sermon, 'Open your eyes, the light is on'. "Have you ever been through something and you say never again for me? If you hadn't learned your lesson it will come again with a different face and name." "Yes, so true! Hallelujah!" Ebony shouted. On numerous occasions she had said that with Lawrence, done that with Malcolm, but it won't be a third time.

Chapter 23

Leaving work, Ebony just kept thinking about what the pastor had spoken on. As the tears ran down her face, she had to figure out what was wrong with her. How could she make this thing stop?

Ebony planned on starting the New Year with new aspirations. Nothing was going to hold Ebony down, so she thought. Not Lawrence or Malcolm with their bullshit. Love and happiness was out there, it just had to find her. The one man that found her and deserved her would indeed get unconditional love.

The flip side was the friendship vs. the romantic interludes. Malcolm was possessive, insecure and needed to dominate. He thought that money was the answer. Ebony needed a man not for the money, but for unconditional love. Quality time is what she desired and enjoyed most.

Malcolm acted like she wanted to pull teeth or something. What was twice a week to watch a movie, eat dinner and make love? It wasn't what he did for her, but to her that was most important. Maybe Malcolm deserved to be with a 'chicken-head' just like Lawrence did. To her it seemed that they didn't know they had a good thing right in their faces.

For the first time in two weeks, Ebony finally broke down. While lying in the bed, she cut the television on to VH1 soul. The channel was playing Monica's videos and wouldn't you know it, "Everything to Me" came on. Ebony started shaking her head, like this can't be happening. A couple of more videos played and then "Love All Over Me" started. This was her and Malcolm's song. The tears streamed down her face. She had that somewhat love she had been trying to capture for years and in a second, it had washed away.

Ebony went into the bathroom and watched the tears. All she could think was you win some and you lose some. She had lost but not on her account.

Trying to mask the pain that led her down this road of self—destruction with abusive relationships, Ebony knew it had to stop. This deadly concoction of abusive behavior, sex, lies and the fantasy of real love had to end somewhere. The cycle had to be broken. No More! Ebony had taken all she was gonna take from any man. Even if this meant she would be by herself in the end.

Something was eating away at her. The cold and the snow really had her mind reeling. Maybe she was glutton for punishment, but something inside of her wanted to reach out to Malcolm. Her better judgment said no, but she dialed the damn phone.

Ebony wanted to let him know that she was having outpatient surgery. The doctor's thought that she might have breast cancer. Ebony wasn't trying to claim anything. Something in her gut wanted this man to know; maybe he would feel some kind of sympathy towards her.

"Hello," Malcolm stated. Ebony could tell that he was sleep and really didn't want to bother him. She explained why she had called and then told him sorry for disturbing his rest. After arriving home, she reflected on why she had called in the first place. Seemed like she couldn't get to sleep and just laid there thinking.

Four o'clock the phone rang. "Are you asleep," Malcolm asked. "No, just laying here," she stated. "My car won't start, would it be too much trouble for you to take me to work?" Without hesitation, Ebony got up and slipped on her boots and coat and drove to Malcolm's house. She tried to explain how she felt about him leaving her shit outside her door. He did agree that he was wrong for that. Malcolm had promised Shawn that they were going to take him to Myrtle Beach when he came back for the summer. The two continued to discuss that on the ride to work.

Malcolm made it there safely, now Ebony had to fight to get her ass back home and get some sleep for work her own fool self. It hadn't even been a good hour after she arrived at work that the phone rang. "You wanna hear something funny? I came home and started my car. It started right up the first go round." Ebony told him that it was the **"Almighty"** trying to tell him something about the relationship, but he wanted to ignore it. Ebony just shook her head. Once again **"GOD"** had the final say.

Ebony thought that the conversation went over pretty well. Shawn was a big boy and if they didn't go to South Carolina, he would understand. She just didn't like to make promises that she couldn't keep. Two hours later as she was checking her email, Malcolm sent her this long drawn out email. "I can't go with you to Myrtle Beach. From the way you talked earlier, you could take it or leave it. It would be best that I not entertain that thought." Enough already!!!!! How much more of this drama was this girl gonna keep taking?

Chapter 24

The following day like clockwork, he started in with more bullshit. Ebony didn't want to argue, her body and her mind was drained. She wouldn't do it! She shut her phone off and went back to sleep. Finally waking up, she had tons of messages and emails. Delete!!! The phone rang and once again it was on. "I don't need you," Malcolm stated.

"Good, why the fuck are you still calling then? Find someone else to harass then. You only call to fucking argue. Is that what you call love? Everything that my ex-husband did to me, you did it in eight months. You are no better than him in my book." Ebony had enough and threw the phone across the room. She thought she had broke it.

As she walked down in the basement, the phone started ringing again. *I wish I would answer that motherfucker.* Just that quick, once she made her way back upstairs, there was a voicemail. "I really need you. My brother just died." If his ass could be stubborn, so the fuck could she. *Oh well*, she thought.

Ebony picked the phone up and called her girl at work to cackle. She began to tell her what Malcolm did and what had just happened. "Ebony, you really need to go be with him. You know you still love him." Deep inside it was true. All the pain he caused, she decided to take her co-worker's advice.

Ebony tried to stick with Malcolm during his hour of grief, but it was going to be a hard task. She had made it to his mother's house and held him tight. This girl was doing everything humanly possible to console this man.

After this funeral, this is it! Ebony called to find out the arrangements. Malcolm thanked her for being in his corner. She thought that's what lover's did, maybe she was wrong.

The day of the service, Ebony was sharp as a tack. His family had only seen her in jeans and a hat, but never decked out. Ebony came clean and did it up. She pulled out the fur coat and hat. It's a small world, she ran into her aunt and cousin or her father's side. Ebony hadn't seen them since her father's mother had passed away. That's been years.

Ebony was surprised after the service was over. Malcolm introduced her to his sister from out of town. He told Ebony that she really looked nice. It had been a long time since she heard that out of his mouth. Malcolm's mother asked if she was coming to the repast. Ebony declined because she had to work.

On her way to work, Malcolm called her. The family was just leaving the cemetery. He knew she was going to want some food, but she never asked because he always said no to everything. The shocker was a couple hours later; he called and told her to come outside. He had brought her plates of food. She was also shocked when he leaned in and kissed her.

Since the incident, he had been calling her to keep her abreast of everything. She had no problem being his sounding board in the time of need. Everyone needed it sometimes. He even came over to the house and made love to her. And yes, her ass was shocked.

The two had planned on going to a concert the following month. Ebony didn't have a problem with going. Something would go wrong;

she could bank on that for sure. The beginning of the month had rolled around and sure enough, his mood swings.

"Did you pencil me in for the date to the KEM concert?" Once again, he on that bullshit. *When we were just friends there was no problem penciling his ass in. Since we have become more then that, he at it again.* If that was the way he was playing it, Ebony had other things that were going to be on her agenda that particular day. He could take whoever he wanted too. It sure as hell wasn't going to be her.

It was like she was planning on leaving his ass at the altar. Ebony made arrangements to go to Charlestown the day of the concert. She had a coupon to stay for dirt cheap and she needed to exhale anyway.

Calgon couldn't do the trick this time, but someone name Maze could. Since the incident in November, Maze finally gave Ebony a chance at redemption. She had promised that she was gonna make it up, but damn! This long. Ok, then she was gonna pull out all the stops this time. Malcolm had fucked her plan up the first time, but not this time.

Ebony arrived home from work and grabbed the chair from the dining room. She took it upstairs to the bedroom and placed it in the center of the floor. Awaiting Maze's arrival, she ran downstairs and ironed her costume and grabbed her high heel boots for the night's events. All the classes she had taken at XPose, she was ready to put it in action and get her money's worth tonight.

Chapter 25

The doorbell rang and Ebony got excited. She ran downstairs and greeted him with a big hug. It had been four months of the charade. Time to put in work. As he walked up the stairs, Ebony flicked the lights on to show him her new hair style. Maze hadn't seen her since she had cut off all her hair. "I like it."

As he glanced into the room and saw the chair, Ebony stated "Wanna try something different tonight." "Hell to the yes," he stated. He quickly got out of his clothes and jumped in the shower. The butterflies were trying to kick in, but she wasn't having that shit tonight. Ebony was going to set the shit in motion and work that body like she never did before.

Maze laid on the bed and lotioned his body as Ebony took a shower. Once she was finished, she snuck downstairs and put on her outfit. Walking up the stairs, she yelled "Close your eyes, here I come."

Once he opened his eyes, he was beside himself. "Oh shit!" Ebony had him sit in the chair as the music began. Her eyes closed and she got into her zone. She whined her body to R. Kelly's "Seem Like Your Ready". Ebony must was twirking it right, his dick was moving from side to side like a thermometer going hot to cold.

Since he was so excited this made her want him more and more. She hopped down on his dick and began to work it for dear life. As it began to get good to the both of them, Maze placed her on the bed. He raised her boots high in the air, and went deep into her opening. The pleasure and the pain of him deep stroking her insides, felt damn good. Before you knew it, both of them were cumming at the same time. Wow!!!!

The two went one more round that night. Maze asked, "Did I hurt you?" "No darling, just hadn't had it like that since I last seen you. You giving up on me early tonight," she said. "That first nut took something out of me." Ebony laid in his arms and felt comforted from the stress she had been enduring.

Two weeks later her and an old classmate, went to Charlestown. They both needed to exhale about men problems. The drive was peaceful and they just needed to vent. After arriving, the two checked in. The hotel was really nice, very lavished. Ebony needed a drink and to start gambling. Off the girls went.

Ebony was on a roll, she was winning like crazy. The two had stayed there for two hours when Quetta got sleepy and decided to go back to the room. They both were knocking down drinks like they were in competition with one another, trying to drown out their problems. The only thing that stopped Ebony was it was too damn cold in there. She caught the bus back to the room. The trip was a success and the two planned on doing it again real soon.

The following week, Ebony was at work and she was craving for crabs. Ebony never ate crabs til the summer and it was not even spring yet. Something had to be wrong with her. She thought in the back of her mind, *naw can't be*. Tina another co-worker went with her to Rite-Aid.

While Ebony was in Rite-Aid, Tina went to grab the food they had purchased. Ebony made sure she got a three pack of pregnancy tests. Sitting out in the car waiting for Tina to come back, Ebony just started thinking, *Damn, girl. What if?*

As Tina approached the door with the food, the fried chicken smell hit Ebony's stomach. She knew then, she was with child . . . .

Discussion Questions

Why did it take Ebony so long to leave Lawrence?

What made her tolerate the abuse from Lawrence and Malcolm?

How did Malcolm play a role in Ebony's quest for love?

Do people believe that saying, what don't kill you only makes your stronger?

Do you think Ebony had a lot of tragedy in her life? What makes so much tragedy happen to one person?

Do you think Ebony handled each situation appropriately? If yes, why? If no, why?

What lessons have you learned as a reader by reading this novel? Have it opened your eyes to what not to fall for in relationships? Discuss

Words of Encouragement

All the time I was going through my trials and tribulations, it only made me closer to **GOD**. Granted I would cry out a many of nights, "Why me?" Later through the years as I had grown, I thought long and hard about the question. The answer was "Why not me?" If **HE** gave it to me, apparently I could handle it. Reflecting back on my life and the abuse I had endured, I was just put here on earth to help the next person; to spread the word about how it drew me nearer to the **most high**.

Each year I have a favorite song that touches my life. This year, I would like to acknowledge Vashawn Mitchell's "Nobody Greater". Truthfully there is nobody greater than **GOD**. I have been on a journey to find that missing love all my life. The conclusion is that **GOD's** love has always been there all the time. When man couldn't or wouldn't do it. Never give up! Trust in the "**Most High**" and always believe that **HE** will make a way out of no way.

Daddy's Girl

I always wanted to be a daddy's girl, but that never would be,
Daddy took that joy away from me,
Couldn't he see I longed for his love from young to old?
Why he had to always be so damn cold,
I look just like him and that ain't no lie,
He always kept me at a distance, I often times cried,
The woman I turned out to be, you should be proud,
You only seemed to notice when you are in a crowd,
That's my daughter my very first born,
But can't you realize how much I am torn,
Apart of me still loves you, I hope and wish, you will love me too!

Broken & Revived

You said you'd love me til death do us part
But now you are tearing things all apart!
Did you want me just to make me blue?
You are not a real man, you had no clue!
You don't beat on something you claim you love.
You suppose to cherish it like a pure dove.
You tried to break me, but I would not bend.
Now you are left standing stupid to pretend.
Your abuse only made me stronger,
I found love in myself that lasts longer,
Because of you, I am much better
I have begun to be a trend setter.
To help let the world know that domestic violence is not to be
endured,
So we as women will not tolerate it for sure.

Lovin You

I am a fragile flower withering cause of life's pain.
I cry so much sometimes I just wish it would rain.
You'll never know how I let my guard down for you.
Because technically I thought you really loved me too!
You played with my heart and tore it all apart.
I gotta find a way to make this brand new start.
I showed myself what love was and that was no lie.
I gave my all to you, nearly felt like I was gonna die. Learning to love
myself, helped me love you.
But now what more could I do.
You wanted it to end cause of your childish ways.
You had me wasting my time for all them days.
It hurts, but I know now what I must do.
Stick to my word and forget all about you.

Letting Go

Letting go I must do to heal the pain in my heart,
Letting go of the past hurt for a fresh new start,
Letting go to let the Master take control of me,
In time HE will reveal and let me see,
The love I've been searching for all this time, was right in my face,
HE was always mine,
All I had to do was call on HIS name,
Because basically my Lord never changes,
HE is always the same.

Available now